O

Gretta Allison [...] artist, writer and [...] lived in a cabin [...] British Colombia and learned how to chop wood, haul water and look a moose in the eye. Art college led to a career of theatre and dance, children's workshops, festivals, and touring with two solo shows. She was discovered while working as a clown on the streets of New York by her future husband, Allen Sabinson, who liked her stories. They now live in California with their daughters Juliana and Elena, their five cats, one dog, three fish and a turtle. They see dolphins in the morning, deer in the evening and movie stars in the afternoon. Life is still an adventure.

This book is dedicated to my mother,

Sally Brigham Keene

Word queen,
Letter-writer,
Bookworm,
Story-teller.
Loud laughing,
Deep sighing,
Life loving,
Memory keeper.

Thanks for being my Mom.

Acknowledgements

First books require many thanks.

Many years ago, Jane Yolen believed I could "Touch magic and pass it on". I clung to her words.

Garth Williams, my childhood idol and inspiration, viewed my drawings with enthusiasm and commanded me, "Stop hiding your portfolio!" I followed his advice.

Paula Danziger read my manuscript while in the bath-tub and said, with her hair still wet, "I'll make a few calls." They were good calls.

My editors, Victoria Eldon and Marion Lloyd gave praise for what they liked and notes I could follow. The story improved.

My family, my friends and members of the various writing groups, all put up with endless rewrites and ragged first drafts. Now they get to read the book.

To all of them and all of you, I offer thanks.

Over the Wall

Gretta Allison

MACMILLAN CHILDREN'S BOOKS

First published 1995 by Macmillan Children's Books

a division of Pan Macmillan Publishers Limited
Cavaye Place London SW10 9PG
and Basingstoke

Associated companies throughout the world

ISBN 0 330 33015 2

9 8 7 6 5 4 3 2 1

A CIP catalogue record for this book is available from
the British Library

Phototypeset by Intype, London
Printed and bound in Great Britain by
Cox & Wyman Ltd, Reading, Berkshire

CONTENTS

Chapter 1
WALLS

"Stupid! Stupid! Stupid! Dumb!" Rachel kicked the pile of leaves that huddled by the high stone wall. The late summer sycamore smelled of coming autumn and pumpkin pies. But Rachel didn't care.

"I hate this stupid place. I want to go home."

Thick, smothering ivy draped the long, high wall. Thin tendrils lifted out from the heavy cloak of leafy green. Thin fingers like those Rachel was used to seeing, pointing, laughing at her, making her want to run away, run home. But not here, she thought. I'd never want to run back here. The wall was long and high, and the pines behind the wall were higher still and dwarfed the brown neglected house Rachel was supposed to now call home.

"But it isn't!" Rachel declared. "It isn't home!"

Home to her was still the fifth floor apartment in the city where she had lived the last year and a half. Early this morning, Rachel and her family had loaded everything they owned into her father's company truck and their new, hardly-been-used 1950 green Chevy station-wagon. Her mother would need a car now they were going to live in this small boring town that didn't even have public transport.

"I'll be doing the errands on my own," her mother had explained to the car dealer last week. "My husband used to be home a lot, but now he has a sales job and travels most of the week." Rachel had seen how her father longingly eyed a rebuilt racing car while her mother talked to the dealer about more practical vehicles. "It's sometimes hard with the new baby and all," her mother had admitted. Rachel was surprised her painfully shy mother had told so much. Usually it was her father who did the talking. But then, everything seemed to be changing.

"Well, Mrs Szeghetti, I have the car for you!" the dealer had announced with salesman enthusiasm. "A nine-year-old Chevy, and, would you believe – not a bit of rust!"

Rachel's father had looked up from the sports car and declared with equal mock astonishment, "My goodness! My daughter is nine as well, and also has not a bit of rust – that is if you don't count her hair!"

Rachel had cringed. She hated when he made dumb jokes in public. Especially about her hair. Her mother and she used to laugh when it was just the three of them: then she didn't mind when he called her "Rusty Red" or some other silly name. She would pull his moustache and tease him back. But that was private. She had seen the rolled eyes and sneering whispers and knew some people thought he was a jerk. The salesman hadn't seemed to notice. He had just wanted to make the sale.

They had bought the Chevy wagon and had packed it this morning with the last scattered items that wouldn't fit in the borrowed truck. Rachel's father was impatient to get to the new town, so her mother agreed to finish the odds and ends while he drove on ahead. As her mother handed in the keys to the landlord and wrote a note to the postman, Rachel stood alone in her empty room. She touched the rainbow that had faced her bed and whispered a last goodbye.

Soon someone would cover over the flowers, sun and rainbow she and her mother had worked so hard to paint. Soon someone else's furniture and belongings would fill the room. Her friends, Mr Mahoney and his roof-top pigeons, and Miss Lenore and her stringy Pekinese would all be friends to someone else.

"They won't remember us," Rachel had confided to her cat, Stripy. "They'll forget we were ever here."

No one called out, "Don't forget to write!" as her mother put baby Matthew into his car bed and tucked Clownie by his cheek. No one but Rachel heard her mother take a deep breath and say with forced gaiety, "Here goes nothing!" as the old car clicked, vibrated and began to roar. No one was there to wave goodbye. Miss Lenore liked her "beauty sleep" and Mr Mahoney needed to get through his morning paper, and the kids in the neighbourhood, well, they had never been Rachel's friends. On the drive through endless country roads, Rachel didn't cry, but instead, pressed her face against the glass and watched the familiar cityscape turn to rolling hills and narrow, winding roads.

"PENNYVILLE!" she had muttered, reading the sign as they entered the town. "It even sounds stupid!"

"Give this place a chance," her mother had said as she pointed out the charms of the grey stone courthouse and the sparse old-fashioned shops in the centre of town. "Isn't it pretty!" she exclaimed as they drove down meandering streets with old trees so tall the branches on either side touched in the middle. They had followed directions and driven beside the long, high wall that stretched along the street opposite an iron-gated park. They turned the corner and found the company truck with boxes piled nearby. Rachel's mother excitedly bundled baby Matthew out of the car and hurried on to the porch. "Come see!" she called, before disappearing into the house.

Rachel stood by the high wall, kicking leaves and viewing her new home with disgust. The dark brown house, with its wraparound porch, was grim and silent. Curled shingles covered the roof like scales on a dragon's back.

"I hate you, dirty old house. I hate everything in this dumb old town." Rachel chewed the tip of her pigtail as she carried Stripy in his carrying case across the weed-filled lawn.

Mr Szeghetti popped out the front door wiping his bushy moustache with a large white handkerchief. He saw Rachel and bowed low, flourishing the cloth.

4

"Welcome," he said with a grin. "Excited?"

"I guess," grumbled Rachel, entering the gloomy front hall. "Can I let Stripy out?"

"Only if you put him in your room," said her mother, brushing a cobweb from a window. "And shut the door until we finish unloading. His litter box is in the kitchen. You must be *very* careful not to let him outside for at least a few days or he might run away."

"I know, Mom. We've only moved a million times before." She lifted Stripy out of his case and kissed his soft orange fur.

Mrs Szeghetti wiped her hands. "But this is different. This is a nice, wholesome town with lovely, sweet children and lots of fresh air. We've lived in city apartments, never in a place like this!"

"That's for sure," Rachel muttered.

Her father playfully pulled her pigtail. "I dropped off your papers at your new school. Looks great. Big playground. And you've only missed the first three weeks. They started fifth of September."

"You're going to make so many new friends tomorrow," added Mrs Szeghetti. "Children in small towns aren't so tough. Won't it be nice to play with friends your own age for a change?"

"No. This place is creepy."

Mrs Szeghetti sighed and rubbed Stripy's head. "I've got to feed Matthew. Your room is upstairs. You might change your mind."

"Can I go for a walk afterwards?" Rachel asked, wanting to flee the gloom. "Just down the street?"

5

"You don't know your way around—" began her mother.

"Let her take a walk, Meg," said her father. "Be good for her."

"But, Alfred . . . oh, OK. Just don't go far and *please* don't even approach the wall next door," Mrs Szeghetti warned. "The rental firm gave strict instructions that our neighbour is *never, ever* to be disturbed. They were quite adamant. Nervous, actually."

"Why?" asked Rachel.

"You know how people exaggerate. They said she was a crazy old witch, protective of her privacy. Go on now. Go see your room."

A witch, thought Rachel as she touched the coiled, snake-smooth banister, saw how it slid atop the railings and formed a balcony above the first floor. She squeezed Stripy tighter as she trudged upstairs past the panelled walls, the stairs creaking as her feet pressed into the blood-red carpet. The air smelled musty, like old clothes and spoiled fruit. She peeked into what she thought must be her parents' room and saw, next door, crib and baby toys. In the bathroom, the bathtub stood on lion claws, and the toilet had a chain hanging from a tank near the ceiling.

"This place is nuts," she declared, following the slim beacon of light that shone down the hall, peeping from under the final portal. Rachel stood before the closed door, hesitated, then turned the dull brass knob.

"Oh, Stripy! Look!" There was her blue-flowered quilt flung across her bed. Boxes marked "R" were piled nearby. All her things that had filled apartment after apartment, from city to city, were here – but contained in one corner of an enormous, light-spattered room. "It's like a beautiful tree house!" One half of the back wall was windowed with small panes of glass. Dust particles swirled in the streaming light. If I had a friend, thought Rachel, we could dress in scarves and dance and swirl. We could sit by the window and tell secrets as if we were birds in the tree. I'll move my bed near the window, and if she's a good friend, she might even sleep over and we'll giggle and count stars as we fall asleep. Maybe. If I ever have a friend.

Rachel hugged her cat and stared past branches of an enormous oak, over the high stone wall to the elaborate roof-top and turrets of the hidden neighbouring mansion. That wall's not so high, thought Rachel. I've climbed on fire escapes much higher than that.

Like a shot, a flock of crows exploded out from pointy pine boughs, circled and swooped around the mansion's roof with its topping of black iron lace. "Caw!" they screamed, then just as suddenly disappeared into the tightly pressed branches. A single crow remained, drifting in the sky. Rachel watched the black mark grow larger, closer, until it landed on a branch near her window. Stripy arched his back and hissed. Rachel could see the huge crow's bright eye and hard, sharp beak.

"Ouch!" Rachel yelped as Stripy's claw dug her arm, but she clutched him closer as if there were no glass between them and the evil-looking bird. "A real witch," she whispered. "You must never go over the wall."

As if in answer, Stripy leaped from her arms, raced along the hall and down the stairs. Rachel hurried after, through the dining-room filled with boxes and into the kitchen. Stripy was scratching, meowing at the back door.

"No!" Rachel yelled, still shaking, remembering the crow's unblinking glare. "You can't go out." Rachel closed the door to the dining-room, then rummaged in some boxes for cat food. "I'll get you something to eat." Suddenly, there came a horrible screeching from the yard.

"Stay," she commanded, holding Stripy with her foot, unlocking the heavy back door, then slipping by the screen.

She jumped down the porch steps. A squirrel and the crow were having a wild disagreement in the branches of the giant oak. "Caw! Caw!" sneered the crow, flying back over the wall.

Rachel looked up at the ancient oak with its deep-ridged corduroy of bark. A leaf let go its hold and spiralled down. Rachel reached out her hand and caught the fluttering red chance to wish. She closed her eyes and concentrated extra hard. "A friend. I wish I had a real friend." She sighed and surveyed the drab yard. "At least you're better than the playground with the broken glass," she told the discouraged-looking bushes. She felt the leaf in her hand and noticed the yellow spot near its centre formed a perfect heart shape. "Now *you* are *really* beautiful," Rachel declared, smoothing the slight curl of its edges, then

8

putting the leaf safely in her pocket. "I'm going to keep you for ever, right next to the four-leaf clover in the dictionary."

The screen door banged. A streak of orange whizzed by.

"Stripy!" She sprang, grabbed for his tail. He darted under the house between a gap of wooden slats, criss-crossed like the tops to cherry pies. Rachel flopped down and peered through the hole. "You bad cat! Come back!"

She wiggled through the broken slats, searching the dark. Green eyes glowed deep within the black. "Stripy. You're gonna get me in big trouble if they know I let you out." She crawled deeper. Something slimy squirmed in the damp ground and her head cracked against a low beam.

"Maybe there are buried bodies, guarded by rats. Maybe those are rats' eyes and not Stripy's at all. Maybe the witch—" A sticky, soft spider's web wrapped across her face. Images of poisonous spiders, hungry for blood, dangled in her brain. She knew you could swell up and die from Black Widow bites.

"I can see you, you jerky cat! Come out of there!" She reached towards Stripy, then saw the mouse gripped in his jaws. "Let go!" Rachel cried. "You're hurting it!"

Stripy made a wild dash as Rachel scrambled after, into the glaring light. Squinting, she caught the last glimpse of Stripy, mouse hanging from his mouth, as he bounded up the ivy and over the witch's wall. "No! Stripy! Not there!"

Tugging her braid, she pleaded, "Please! Please!

9

Come back!" The familiar hollowness swelled inside, as she thought of Stripy gone for ever.

The witch, she thought. The witch is there. I don't care. I'm not scared of any stupid old witch. She remembered how in the city, the drunk with the dirty face and the swollen eye had grabbed her arm and she had kicked him and run away. No one can scare me. With a glance to make sure her mother wasn't watching, Rachel jumped and grasped on to the mesh of ivy and dug her shoes into the cracks between the stones. Hand over hand, she pushed and pulled until her legs were straddling the top of the wall. She caught her breath and looked into the garden below. Stripy was crouching in the grass playing with the mouse.

Rachel slipped down the wall, landing on the ground with a thud. She spun around, seeing if anyone was there who would have heard her fall. Only a faint breeze rustled the nearby branches. Stripy, however, grabbed the mouse back in his jaws and bounded away. Rachel followed, wishing the crisp fallen leaves were not announcing her every step. I think I've heard that witches have very sensitive hearing. But maybe this one is old and doesn't.

"Come here, you stupid cat," she whispered as she finally cornered him, his tail switching as he crouched beside a fish pond.

"Let the mouse go!" Rachel ordered, speaking so low that even a very alert witch wouldn't hear. Reluctantly, Stripy dropped his prize and gave his fur two self-conscious licks. Rachel grabbed for him, but he ran, skittering back over the wall. The mouse cowered in the corner, shaking.

Cautiously, Rachel scooped the creature into her hand. "Poor thing!" She stroked the silky fur and curled the long tail around its warm little body. "You have tiny round ears, like in cartoons!" Rachel felt the mouse quiver, its breath rapid, heart pounding. "I'm sorry Stripy hurt you. Sometimes he's a bad cat, but I'll keep you safe, little Mousie. I know you're scared."

Rachel sat on the edge of the pond. "I'll get a cage and build a castle with windows you can peek from." She gently rubbed between its ears. "I'll buy a running wheel and you'll tickle me with your whiskers and play hide-and-seek. I always wanted a mousie just like you. Maybe you are my new friend. I wished for a friend." She sang: "Mousie, Mousie. You're my mousie. I will build a little housie—"

"Who are you?" said a crackling voice. "And what are you doing in my garden?"

Chapter 2
MAGIC

Rachel gasped. Before her stood the witch. She wore a long, black, high-necked dress and her white hair was pulled tight in a bun. She leaned on a gold-topped cane.

"Well," snapped the witch, her pale blue eyes glittering, two fires amid a mass of wrinkles. "Answer me!"

"I – I – I'm sorry," Rachel stammered, staring at the face, so very white and wrinkled, like tissue wrapping paper used too many times.

The witch came closer. "What do you have there?"

Rachel reluctantly opened her hand. "My mouse," she whispered. "Stripy, my cat, he caught it. We live next door."

The witch peered at the tiny animal. "Hmnpf. So

you are the ones renting the Caretaker's House." Her long bony finger pointed at the mouse. "He's hurt, give him to me."

Rachel clasped the mouse. I'm not going to let an old witch have him! She probably wants him for stew. "He's mine!" Rachel said defiantly.

The witch pursed her lips and glared at Rachel. "What a presumptuous little girl! Give it to me immediately!" Her hand reached for the mouse but Rachel held it against her chest and took a step back. She probably collects snakes and toads as well, thought Rachel. But I can run away. Unless she does something – something magic – like freeze me with a spell or turn me into a frog! That would be sort of interesting . . .

The witch, vibrating with fury, whipped her cane up and directed the tip at Rachel. "How dare you disobey me!" She spat the words through yellowed teeth. "You are an impudent brat trespassing on *my* private property. You have allowed *your* nasty cat to injure a helpless creature and now you are refusing to allow me to see if I can save its tenuous life. I have never met such a selfish, insolent child!"

Save its life? Maybe my mouse is hurt really bad, thought Rachel. And it *is* my fault. If I hadn't left the back door open, Stripy would never have caught him. Maybe this witch can do good spells. Rachel slowly extended her cupped hands towards the old woman.

The witch pursed her lips, leaned over and ran her finger along the mouse's back. "Hmnpf." Her tight frown shifted the network of ancient wrinkles. "I had hoped it was merely in shock, but its spine is broken."

"Can you fix it?" Rachel asked.

The old lady shook her head. "It will soon die."

Just then the mouse writhed and emitted a soft squeak. Rachel saw a drop of blood oozing through its fur. "Mousie!" she cried and dropped to her knees, cradling the tiny creature. "Oh, Mousie! I'm sorry! I'm sorry my cat bit you! I wanted to take care of you! I wanted to be your friend. I'm sorry!"

The old woman leaned with both hands on her cane and watched with embarrassed amazement at the little girl sobbing at her feet. "Now, now," she muttered. "You'll make yourself sick with all that sobbing."

"I don't care," Rachel wailed. "I don't care if I die too! I do everything wrong! And I hate it here! I didn't want to move! It's all stupid and dumb!" She looked at the little mouse as its chest beat rapidly and its eyes stared wildly up at her. "He was going to be my friend." She whispered, "Please get better. Don't really die."

The old lady fingered the cameo brooch pinned to her collar. "My goodness! There is no need to carry on so! I'm sure you will make plenty of friends with playmates at school. You'll soon forget this little mouse."

"That's not true! What do you know? Kids are mean! They call me names and do stupid things! I hate going to school!" Rachel rubbed her nose on her arm. "Stripy's my only friend."

"I see." The old lady sighed and eased herself down by the edge of the pool. Silently she stared at the fish swimming in the water, then like a queen, she lifted

14

her head high and spoke. "Bring the mouse here."

Rachel's lip quivered. Maybe she could make him better. Maybe she has healing potions. The old lady dipped a handkerchief edged with lace into the water, then squeezed a drop near the tiny mouth. The mouse did not blink.

"Was that magic?" Rachel asked. "Will he get well?"

The old lady sighed. "My dear, comfort him. Tell him he's been a good mouse, lived bravely and ended life with a friend. That's more than many can say."

A crow lighted on a branch. "Caw! Caw!" he cried.

The old lady smiled at the crow. "Yes. It's unusual to see a stranger in the garden. Unfortunately, we are in the midst of a sober situation. Your usual levity will not be appreciated." The crow cocked his head with an intelligent look, nodded, then flew off to a nearby pine.

Rachel gasped. "You *are* magic! You talk to crows!"

"Only if they talk to me first." The old lady grasped the golden knob of her cane and leaned towards Rachel. "My dear, there are all kinds of magic. What makes a mouse run and squeak and you talk and ask difficult questions?"

"That's just life."

"Aah. Just life, you say. But even after death, life's force remains. Some say it's energy, others soul. I call it magic. Death is part of the cycle."

"He's dying. That's what you're saying. Isn't it?"

The old lady nodded.

Rachel lifted the mouse close. In a shaky whisper,

15

she sang: "Mousie, Mousie. Sleep, my mousie. My hands will be your little housie."

The small mouse body shuddered, then relaxed, motionless, still. Rachel felt the limp weight of a creature that had been alive and now was not.

The old lady lifted the mouse from Rachel's hands, wrapped the body in her lace-edged handkerchief and laid it on the fountain edge. "The mouse is gone. Only his body is left, and he doesn't need that anymore." The pool rippled from a sudden breeze. "Thunderstorm blowing in. Come. Give me a hand. It's much easier getting down than up, and at my excessively old age, nothing is easy."

Rachel took hold of the thin, black arm and pulled.

"Stop!" commanded the old lady, with a fearsome face. "My arm is not a parsnip waiting to be yanked!" Noting Rachel's look of horror, she added: "Child, roast little girl has never been my diet. Come close."

Grasping Rachel's shoulder, the old lady heaved herself to standing. "Cursed be this infernal damp which makes my bones ache so!" She lifted her cane and pointed the way down a slate path. "Walk slowly, my dear. I have a plan. Where we are going is not far, but I'm afraid you must act as pallbearer and carry the deceased."

She talks funny, thought Rachel as the old lady's hands dug into her shoulder, and they followed the winding path. I don't always understand what her words mean but I know what she's saying. The huge grey mansion loomed past rows of late-blooming roses and flowers gone to seed. What a strange place. My mom would have a fit if she knew I was here. But at least it's not as bad as when I had all those candles in the abandoned building and the fireman brought me home.

"We have reached our first destination!" announced the old lady, standing before a stone shed. Like a gnome house! thought Rachel. They shuffled through the shadows. Silhouettes of shovels, rakes and old-fashioned tools sprouted from the corners, and rafters were hung with faded bouquets. The old lady tugged open a drawer and pointed to what appeared to be a bunch of onions. "Choose one firm and vital," she ordered. "Choose one bursting with dormant life."

Amid crackling paper skins, Rachel found a smooth one with a tiny green point. Maybe they're magic, she thought. She's going to bring the mouse back to life!

"Perfect," declared the old lady. "Now we will continue our journey." She no longer leaned on Rachel but led the way with slow determined steps.

They meandered through the labyrinth of unclipped hedges, crumbling planters and statues streaked with mould, stopping at last in front of a red-tinged maple. A bird-bath with a plump, winged cherub stood nearby.

"Choose a spot and dig," the old lady commanded, handing Rachel a rusted trowel.

As Rachel knelt on the ground, the old lady muttered, "Such sad ruin. So long since I've been to the far garden. The robins always came first to this bird-bath, when it was clean, not filled with muck. Nice for a little girl to come in spring and—" The old lady returned from her distant gaze. "Little girl!" she said sharply. "I don't even know your name."

"My name is Rachel," Rachel replied, standing up from her digging. "Is this deep enough?"

"Yes, yes, deep enough," the old lady said, suddenly impatient. "Place the mouse in the ground, then the bulb, pointed end up. Pat the dirt firmly in place. I suppose I must relinquish my good handkerchief, but no matter."

Rachel tenderly placed the mouse in the shallow grave, then clutched the bulb and said softly, "I thought there'd be magic."

"Magic! Well, it is magic." The old lady steadied herself on her cane. "One spring day, when the snow has gone, a tulip will bloom, radiant with the spirit of your mouse."

"Oh." Rachel bit her lip. "But – I don't want to say goodbye – and have it be for ever. I want something to make it all OK. I want my mouse."

"Child – Rachel. Life is long and will always give sorrow. When I was a girl, about your age, I lost—" The old lady paused, then awkwardly touched Rachel's shoulder. Rachel felt her tremble as she spoke. "When we can no longer see those we love, we think them gone. It is the same with tulips. They grow, bloom, a moment of glory – then, petals fall, leaves shrivel and die. We forget the tulip bulb – alive, but hidden, waiting." Rachel laid the bulb in the hole.

"You know," the old lady continued, "I cried when my kitten died. My father – I suppose he was feeling as helpless as I feel now – he comforted me by planting a small rose-bush where we buried Mr Puss. In spring, every rose felt like a part of my beloved kitten."

Rachel looked up at her. "Do you still have that rose-bush?"

"I do indeed. For any creature I love who departs this world, I plant a flower. Each spring life bursts forth with flowers and memories." Eyes shining, the old lady's pale face turned almost rosy. A drop of rain landed on Rachel's hand and a few more dotted the ground. Thunder shook the darkening sky. "Trust the magic. Say goodbye."

Comforted, but with a dull ache inside, Rachel pushed the dirt over the small white shroud and tulip bulb. "Goodbye, Mousie," she murmured. Wiping her eyes with her muddy hand, she added, "I won't forget you."

"Come." The old lady motioned. "You should run home. The back wall door is nearby and leads to the empty lot around the corner from your house."

They made their way through the garden to a narrow wooden door set in the high stone wall. Rachel smiled, suddenly shy. "You know my name, but I don't know yours."

"Hmnpf. I suppose you may call me Miss B. That's what the children used to—" Her face changed. It seemed to fill with terrible pain and she suddenly snapped, "You must never, do you understand, *never*, tell *anyone* you were here."

Rachel shrank from the anger in her voice, but nodded, remembering other secrets she had kept. Mom gets too upset, she rationalized. Dad says her nerves are strung too high. It's better when I keep things to myself. "I won't tell," she promised. "But can I come back sometimes? At least when my mouse-tulip blooms?"

"I don't know. Sam and I have managed quite well without — we are not used to—"

"Who is Sam?"

"Sam is Sam. I will not be interrogated further. Go!"

Why is she so upset, thought Rachel. Why does she want everything secret? What's the big mystery? Rachel pulled the leaf from her pocket.

"Here. You can have my special leaf. See the heart-shaped spot of yellow? I was going to keep it for ever, but I want you to have it instead."

The old woman took the leaf. Her face softened. "I will treasure it always," she solemnly replied.

"Caw!" called the crow as he watched from his perch in the tall pine.

"You had better skedaddle before you get soaked," said Miss B, opening the door. She seemed to be smiling as she adjusted her brooch.

Rachel ran home. SLAM! BANG! In through the back door.

"Rachel!" exclaimed her mother. "Where have you been? We found Stripy outside, meowing on the porch. I thought I told you not to let him out! And you were gone so long. I was worried sick! I thought—"

"Now, Meg," Rachel's father cajoled. "All's well that ends well." He winked at Rachel. "Your buddy is in the living room."

Rachel found Stripy curled on the sofa. She buried her nose in his fur. "The mouse died," she whispered. "You killed him." Stripy stretched and yawned.

"I met the witch and we buried the mouse under a tulip. It made me sad." Stripy began to purr as she scratched his favourite place beneath his neck. "Don't worry. I still love you. But no more mice!"

Chapter 3
AMBASSADORS

"Rachel," her mother called from the foot of the stairs. "You're going to be late for your first day of school."

Rachel leaned over the balcony. "But, Mom, I can't decide if this is the dress I should wear."

"That's fine. It doesn't matter."

"You don't understand," Rachel argued, walking downstairs and buttoning her sleeve at the same time. "What if the kids think I look goofy?"

"You look very pretty," said Mrs Szeghetti, smoothing the stubborn collar. "Hold still and let me braid your hair."

"Maybe I shouldn't wear a dress with a bow," Rachel suggested as her mother wove the two red plaits. "Maybe country kids don't get dressy for school."

"Hold still, or you'll have lopsided braids!"

Rachel rubbed the dirty toe of her clunky shoes against her knee socks. "Maybe I'll bring a skirt and a blouse in a bag. You run in, see what everyone's wearing. If no one's wearing a dress, I can change."

"Rachel, what matters is you, not what you wear."

"I know, but I wish my hair was a pretty colour, just sorta red and wavy. Like yours. I hate being a stupid old 'freckle face' with weird green eyes."

"You aren't stupid, you just need to pay more attention in school and your freckles are cute and I always wanted green eyes instead of blue. So come eat breakfast before it gets cold."

The kitchen smelled of coffee, eggs and burned toast. "Oh, Alfred!" exclaimed Mrs Szeghetti, snatching the charcoaled pieces of bread from the toaster. "You know this old thing has to be watched."

Mr Szeghetti peered out from behind his newspaper. "Apologies, my darling Meg." He looked at Rachel. "A vision of loveliness!" Rachel grinned as her father leaped out of his chair, landed on one knee, and kissed her fingertips. "Could it be – Princess Alexandria from Russia? No. Too young. Must be Princess Fiona of Sweden."

Mrs Szeghetti smiled as she scraped the burned edges of toast. "You and your stories. If she's a princess, who are we? I'm certainly not a queen."

"Her faithful ambassadors," Mr Szeghetti replied, returning to his coffee. "Part of the royal entourage."

"We certainly move enough to be ambassadors,"

agreed Mrs Szeghetti, surveying the unpacked boxes. "Rachel, eat."

"I am. See?" Rachel stuffed an enormous forkful of toast and egg into her mouth, the yellow yolk dribbling down her chin. "What do ambassadors do besides move?"

"They lead a wild, exciting life," her father replied. "Parties and parades with royalty – and sometimes," he lowered his voice, "spying."

"And they live in beautiful embassies," her mother continued, slipping a napkin inside Rachel's lunch box. "Where someone else does the dishes and changes nappies, but where little girls still must go to school. Wipe your mouth and grab your sweater. We're late."

"What do embassies look like?" Rachel asked her father.

"Mansions with secret passages," he replied, sounding mysterious.

Like Miss B's, thought Rachel. She acts like she's met royalty. Maybe she's a spy. "Do spies talk funny?"

"As a matter of fact, one time—"

"Alfred! We don't have time for any more of your stories! Here's Matthew's bottle. We have to *go*! *now*!"

"Bye, Daddy."

"I'm on the road again," said her father, giving her a kiss on the head. "So, see you later, Alligator."

"In a while, Crocodile. Sunday? You'll be back?"

"Sure thing, Shoestring. Sunday. You knock 'em dead, ya hear!"

★

24

The school was built of small, dark red bricks. Rachel counted sixteen steps to the white columned entrance. It sure is prettier than my other schools, thought Rachel. She and her mother's shoes clicked as they hurried through the echoing hall. Mrs Szeghetti stopped at the office to ask instructions.

"You're late," said the woman at the desk. "I'll take her to class."

Rachel hugged her mother extra long. Don't let go. I'm not ready. I'll come back tomorrow.

"Say goodbye to your mother," the woman ordered, then gripped Rachel's hand and led her past closed classrooms and muffled children's voices. "Fourth Grade – Room three zero four," the woman snapped as she opened the door. The class fell silent.

"You must be the new girl," said a cheerful voice. Rachel looked up at a smiling face. "I'm Miss Brigham, your teacher. Now let me see . . . Rachel Szeghetti. Do you say 'Seghetti' or 'Zeghetti'?"

"It's 'S' like 'spaghetti' without the 'P'."

A girl with neat blonde curls said in a loud whisper, "So that's what she has on her head!" Titters sparked around the room. I don't care if they laugh, Rachel told herself. I don't care.

Miss Brigham frowned. "I want you to make Rachel feel at home. Your seat will be in the middle, behind Milly." Miss Brigham directed her to an empty desk. Milly was a stringy-haired girl with glasses. Rachel could feel all the eyes watching as she took her seat. She stole a glance at her neighbours. On one side was the girl with neat blonde curls and on the other side was a boy playing with a plastic dagger.

25

"Now, class," said Miss Brigham. "I want everyone to draw a picture of one of your favourite places. Really use your imagination and think of where you'd like to be right now."

I'll draw my apartment building, Rachel thought, longing for the familiar. She drew a tall building, then added purple flags, pink flowers, and a huge yellow sun. Now it's fancy – like an embassy. The Queen probably visits all the time. With that, she drew a lady with long yellow hair and a blue-green dress, and on top of her head, a huge gold crown. If my parents were ambassadors, we'd meet the Queen. So Rachel drew herself, her father, mother, and Stripy, then remembered she had forgotten baby Matthew.

She sighed. Everything changed when Mom and Dad decided to have a baby, she decided. That's when the talk started about how we needed to settle down and be more "stable". So what if most of Dad's ideas didn't work. She smiled as she remembered the portable pancake stand. Matthew's the problem, she thought as she tried to draw him in her mother's arms. Maybe I could leave him on a doorstep. Rachel thought of the imposing grey stone mansion and Miss B. Wouldn't she be surprised to find a baby trespasser!

The teacher's voice shook away her daydream. "Lessie, would you please collect the pictures," called Miss Brigham. "And Snapper, put that knife away or it's going in my desk."

The girl with the neat blonde curls began gathering pictures. Rachel eyed the girl's ribbon barrettes and expensive ruffled dress and congratulated herself for not wearing a skirt and blouse. But she won't ever be

26

my friend, thought Rachel. She's too pretty and rich.

Lessie came to Rachel and inspected her picture. "What's that?"

Rachel avoided Lessie's eyes. "It's an embassy."

Lessie snatched the picture. "What's an 'embassy'?"

Rachel began putting her crayons back in the box. "It's a fancy house where royalty comes to visit."

"How do you know?"

All that was left was the blue-green crayon. Rachel began peeling its paper. "I used to live there."

Dropping the papers on to the desk, Lessie leaned her face close to Rachel's. "Is that a queen and did you really meet her?"

Rachel took a deep breath. "Lots of times." She rubbed blue smudge off her thumb. "We were ambassadors."

"Lessie," Miss Brigham cautioned. "Enough talking. Please finish collecting the papers."

"Yes, Miss Brigham." Lessie scurried to the next row.

At recess time in the playground, a crowd gathered around Rachel. "Lessie said you lived in a castle called an 'embassy'. Did you live there a long time?" asked a dark-eyed, dark-haired girl named Susan.

"What did the queen look like?" asked Donna, a tall skinny girl with buck teeth.

Lessie put her arm around Rachel's waist. "She had long blonde hair down to her toes. Isn't that right?"

Rachel chewed on her braid and nodded.

A sturdy, compact boy with tousled brown hair

asked, "If you were in an embassy, what country was it?"

"Yeah," said Snapper, waving his plastic knife. "Billy's right. If you were one of those embassy guys, where did you live?"

Lessie and all the children stared at Rachel.

The momentary silence revealed an airplane flying overhead. Rachel swallowed hard. "We moved a lot."

Lessie smiled approvingly. "I'm going to be Rachel's best friend. Anyone else has to be okayed by the Ambassador Friendship Club. Right?"

Rachel, overcome with awe, nodded assent.

Milly jumped up and down, clapping her hands, chanting: "Me too! Me too! Me too!"

Lessie linked her arm through Rachel's. "Ambassadors' daughters don't play with dummies!" she said with disgust, then whispered, "Let's go to the bench and share my candy bar. You don't want creeps like Silly Milly hanging around. She's weird, so the teachers let her do special stuff and dance a lot. My mother says she should be in an institution."

The chocolate oozed down Rachel's throat, as she remembered Milly's grinning face. "Donna and Susan are OK," continued Lessie. "But I'm going to be your best friend."

After school, Rachel found the green station-wagon parked out front. "How was school?" asked Mrs Szeghetti, opening the door.

"Fine," Rachel answered, looking back at the laughing, shouting children, lining up for buses or walking home together. "I think I made a friend."

"Oh Rachel! That's wonderful! I told you it would

28

be easier in a small town. And your teacher?"

"Nice," said Rachel. She saw the smile broaden on her mother's face. I wish cats could come to school, Rachel thought, and held her books tightly in front of her chest.

Chapter 4
LIES

After dinner, Rachel's mother asked her to help bring the empty boxes into the attic. A ladder was set in the upstairs hall underneath a small square door. Rachel lifted each box above her head and passed them to her mother. "Can I come up too?"

"I suppose," replied her mother. "I'm not sure what's up here. Be careful on the ladder."

Faint light drifted in from dormer windows. Signs of mice, like seeds on a bun, lay everywhere. Stacked in haphazard array were sagging boxes and dusty trunks. Her mother cautioned, "Remember, these things aren't ours."

"Whose are they?" asked Rachel, drawing in the dust.

"I don't know. The lawyer who collects the rent

told us only that the house has been empty for years."

"And he said it was really a witch who lives next door?" Rachel ventured.

Mrs Szeghetti's hands fluttered nervously as she brushed back her hair. "Of course not. Witches aren't real. Some old eccentric, I suppose. Maybe some trouble in the past. The chemist didn't believe me at first when I told him our address. Then he looked at me funny, and when I said we were up from the city, he said, 'Well that explains it! Anyone from around here would know better than to live next to *that* place.' So I assume our neighbour must be quite strange and not very friendly."

Rachel thought of Miss B. She's not so strange! She knows a lot and says smart things! If she is a witch, she's a good witch. Rachel almost related her encounter, but decided this was another secret it was best to keep.

Matthew, from his crib, began to cry.

"Oh dear," sighed her mother. "I hoped he'd sleep a little longer."

"Can I stay and look in the boxes?"

"They're horribly dirty!"

"I'll take a bath. I promise. Please?"

Matthew increased his wail.

"All right. But be careful. Just don't touch anything that seems important."

Boards creaked and mouse droppings rattled to the floor as she lifted the lid of the largest trunk.

Pennyville Gazette, read the yellowed newspaper heading, October 14th, 1891. Why would anyone save a trunk of papers? She flipped through the frail pages. I didn't know they had cartoons in the olden days. And they have news drawings instead of photographs, Rachel noted. Seated on a ragged quilt she searched for interesting pictures.

"Bath time!" came the call.

Rachel took a pile of papers, before climbing back down the ladder. She hid them in her wardrobe. "I'm sure it's OK to look at them," she told Stripy as he investigated the smell. "They can't be that important."

On Tuesday Rachel pleaded to wear her pink party dress to school. "But, Mommy! You don't understand! My best friend always wears fancy dresses!" Her mother relented.

"Very pretty!" was Lessie's immediate comment. "I think dresses are much nicer than skirts, don't you?"

"Oh, yes," agreed Rachel. "Much nicer."

"I'm glad our desks are together." Lessie took out a pencil box initialled with gold letters. "My mother says you're renting the Old Caretaker House. Isn't it creepy, next door to the witch?"

"Why do you say she's a witch?"

"Everyone knows!" Lessie whispered: "I heard she burned hundreds of innocent people, but she's rich and didn't go to jail. Instead, there's a curse – she'll never die and always have to remember her terrible deeds!"

That's not true! thought Rachel. It can't be!

Lessie continued. "And there's a monster she keeps chained in a dungeon. The people who deliver their groceries say they've heard him moaning. That's why they just leave the packages on the stairs and run."

Rachel clenched her jaw. *I wouldn't run. I didn't run from Miss B and I wouldn't run from a monster. I'm not scared.*

"Why are you looking like that?" asked Lessie. "I told my parents you were ambassadors. My mother thinks that's *very* exciting. My father says anyone in a foreign office is connected to the secret service. Is that true?"

Rachel adjusted the buckle on her shoe. "Lessie. I've got to explain. We moved a lot, but we didn't exactly live in embassies. My dad travels – sells things. See, I—"

"I understand. Your dad's a spy and sells secrets and you can't let people know. I won't tell anyone. Promise."

"Attention, class!" called Miss Brigham, pointing to the pictures on the bulletin board. "You made such interesting drawings! Lessie drew her ballet class, Milly drew flowers, Billy drew outer space and Snapper drew himself as a cowboy out west with guns he will *not* bring to school – and Rachel, could you tell us about your interesting picture?"

"She lived in embassies all over the world and met queens!" Donna blurted, excitedly waving her arm.

Miss Brigham gave Rachel one of her many smiles.

Rachel felt her shoulders stretch towards her ears as she sank lower into her seat.

"And," whispered Susan, "her father's a spy!"

Rachel looked questioning at Lessie who scribbled on a piece of paper, folded it small and flicked it near Rachel's feet. Rachel ducked down, then opened the note in her lap. "We'll eat lunch together at the corner table. OK?" was written in flawless penmanship.

Somehow Rachel's cucumber sandwich seemed soggier than usual and her apple was full of bruises. Lessie had a handful of bright-coloured candies which she let Rachel eat instead. "Now that you are my best friend," Lessie announced, snapping her lunch box shut, "this is for you." She unfastened her gold locket and handed the necklace to Rachel.

Rachel gingerly held the gold locket and chain. "It's beautiful. You sure your mother won't get mad?"

"Of course not," Lessie replied with a flip of her curls. "She lets me do anything I want."

Rachel gazed at the locket on her desk all afternoon, now and then touching the small gold heart. When it was time to go home, Miss Brigham handed out notices for the Back to School Night when all the parents visited the classrooms. "Return them, signed, as soon as possible. And remember, tomorrow is the reading aptitude test, so get a good night's sleep."

Rachel stuck the notice in her jacket pocket. What if Miss Brigham tells my mother about us being ambassadors? What if Mom gets really mad?

Wednesday she wore her brown jumper. It's not fancy, thought Rachel, but covers the chocolate stains on my lace blouse. The strap on her black party shoes snapped, so she wore her smaller white ones. Lessie would probably laugh at a lace blouse with clunky school shoes.

The reading test was hard. The letters on the page seemed more like shapes than words. Pencils are better for drawing, she thought, wishing she could tear her test, with its sparse answers and elaborate doodles, into tiny pieces. Now Miss Brigham will know I'm stupid and dumb.

The children rushed into the playground after lunch. Lessie handed star badges, cut from silver paper, to "selected members of the Ambassador Friendship Club".

Donna whispered to Rachel, "I was Lessie's best friend last year."

Embarrassed, Rachel looked away from the shiny badge now pinned to Donna's coat. Inwardly she cringed – I wish I was just one of the "girls", not the "ambassador's daughter".

"Donna! Rachel! Come jump rope!" called Susan. Rachel tried, but kept tripping. "My feet hurt," she explained. "I'm going on the swing." She shunned the swing next to Milly, who smiled at her with eager eyes. Milly, alone of all the children, was deemed unworthy of a silver badge. I wish she'd stop grinning with that goofy face! Rachel thought as the rubber seat snugged round.

Rachel pushed the ground – reach, curl quick, stretch, until swing suspended, whoosh the air. She imagined flying above school with its singsong shouting voices, above silver badges flashing in the sun, above the entire town of Pennyville, with all its strangeness and strangers. She imagined Miss B flying, wisps of white hair mingling with clouds. If I were a witch I would fly and fly! I wish I could swing, swing all day! But the recess bell sounded, and school continued.

★

"Guess what!" exclaimed Rachel's mother, as Rachel climbed into the car that afternoon. "I had several calls today from mothers of your new school friends. They've invited me for tea! You've made quite a hit!"

Rachel's skin prickled. She felt the notice in her pocket. Mom can't come to Back to School Night! Not now!

"Anything wrong?" asked Mrs Szeghetti.

The words stuck like swallowed gum. "No, Mommy."

Saturday Rachel slept late, awaking to her mother vacuuming. Two whole days where nothing bad can happen, she thought, and then comes Monday! She dreaded facing Lessie. If her father were here, maybe he could help her think up some interesting story that would get her out of this mess. But he had called and said he was delayed until Wednesday. And besides, then she'd have to tell him what she had done.

Rachel leaned on the windowsill next to her bed and watched the crows flying over the pines in the yard over the wall. Two landed on a branch near a ghostly figure who slowly glided between the trees like a flicker of light. That must be Miss B! Rachel felt warmed by the thought of the old lady and how they had planted the tulip bulb together. She really liked the leaf I gave her, thought Rachel. She didn't think it was silly – I could tell. Old people are easier to talk to than kids. Miss Lenore would let me brush her little dogs and she'd tell me stories about the famous people she met when she was a hairdresser, and Mr Mahoney would read the funny papers with me and then explain which horses he would bet on if he had the money. They'd listen when I'd talk about plans I had or things I'd seen.

Rachel sighed. Whenever her family had moved, it was never the children her own age whom she had missed. I just get on better with people who've been around for a while, concluded Rachel. But Miss B – she seems smarter than any of them, and definitely more – well – *magic*! I bet she would know what to do about Lessie! In an instant Rachel was dressed and downstairs. "I'm going for a walk!" she called, not waiting for a response.

Running around to the empty lot so her mother wouldn't notice, she pressed through tangled bushes to the wall, then dug her fingers into the narrow spaces between the stones. I don't believe the mean things Lessie said about Miss B, she thought as she reached the top. And even if there is a monster, it doesn't *have* to be mean – maybe just interesting, like Miss B! She breathed deep and jumped, landing in late blooming chrysanthemum. Their pungent smell clung as she wandered round the garden looking for her mysterious neighbour.

"I see you have returned!" cackled a familiar voice.

Rachel spun around and noticed a small, round, open building – a porch outside the house. The white paint was peeling but the carved lattice was intact. Miss B was seated inside, this time dressed all in white.

"Well, come in! No sense lallygagging!"

"It's like being inside a bird cage," Rachel commented, sitting on the bench beside Miss B.

"Hmnpf," replied Miss B, smoothing a few fly-away wisps of hair. "I don't feel at all inclined to chirp, so I suggest we communicate by more traditional means. You don't look so chirpy yourself. May I inquire if something's amiss?"

The locket was cold beneath Rachel's shirt. "Yeah. I guess." She sighed and thought it might be better to meet the monster than think about her problems. "It's hard to explain."

"Beginnings are the best place to start," replied Miss B.

Rachel told her story. Miss B tapped on her brooch, then said firmly, "You will not lose a friend if you tell this girl – Lessie – the truth. She is a manipulator – not a friend. I say good riddance!"

"But all the kids listen to her!" Rachel cried. "I'll never make friends if she's my enemy!" Rachel tugged her braid. "My mother always worries," she said softly, "because I'm not good at making friends my own age."

"Nonsense!" replied Miss B. "Friends are not something you concoct with a secret formula – a teaspoon of this, a tad of that! The only friend you *make*, is yourself. And if you like that friend, *yourself*, true friends will like her as well. The rest of the world – well let them be hanged!"

"That's not what I meant by 'making friends'. And you can't 'make' yourself!"

"Of course you can, and will." Miss B sat up very straight. "Birth to death, we are our own inevitable product, our first and final friend."

"But I want to know what to *do*!"

"*Do!?* You know what you must do. There is only

one exit from the maze of lying. You must tell the truth."

Rachel sighed. "That's hard. I'm scared."

Miss B twinkled. "Nonsense. You weren't very scared of me."

"That was different. I'm not scared of *big, unusual*, scary things. Just normal stuff – like kids in school and tests and things like that. Isn't there a magic pill to make everybody forget or a magic perfume I could wear so no one would ever get mad at me?"

"All this talk of magic," muttered Miss B. "And I never thought of myself as big and unusual." She paused. "There is something. Have you ever had a courage stone?" Rachel shook her head. The old lady reached into the pocket of her skirt, then placed a small pale stone in Rachel's palm. "This will be *your* courage stone now."

"What makes it work?"

"Let me see – how to explain? First you must do a courageous act. The courage goes into the stone and – next time your courage will be doubled, and so on and so on. Very helpful, considering, from my experience, life's challenges only get harder."

"This is great! Wow! Thank you," said Rachel, gently stroking the smooth stone. "I guess I'd better be going home."

"I imagine so." An autumn wind blew through the garden as the two walked towards the back wall.

"Use the courage stone well," said Miss B, jiggling the lock of the heavy wooden door.

"Tomorrow I'll tell Lessie the truth," Rachel said,

with a determined tone. "Maybe she'll think it's funny."

"Maybe," rustled the leaves.

"Perhaps," replied Miss B.

Chapter 5
COURAGE

All day Rachel rubbed the courage stone. The smoothness felt comforting, as if somehow she was smoothing all her problems away – eliminating the bumps and rough places in her life. She rehearsed in her mind what she would say. Make it come out right, she told her stone. Make it all be OK. Finally, at lunch time, Lessie went to throw away her milk carton. Rachel quickly followed. Now. She told the stone. Give me courage now.

"Lessie, I have something important to tell you."

"A secret spying mission and you need my help?"

"No. Nothing like that. I want to give back your locket. See, what I was telling you before, well, I—"

"What's the matter? Isn't it good enough? I know the queens must have given you really great stuff, but

41

that locket is fourteen carat gold and my—"

"I love the locket," interrupted Rachel. "It's the most beautiful locket I've ever seen." First she squeezed the courage stone in her pocket, then withdrew the delicate necklace. She placed the locket in Lessie's palm. "But I can't keep it – because – because I—"

"Fine! Just forget it!" Lessie jammed the locket into her pocket, gave a flip of her curls and ran off.

I want to swing and swing, thought Rachel. But when the class reached the playground, the swings were full, so Rachel decided to sit on the bench and wait. The sun shone with Indian summer exuberance. Some of the children shed their jackets and created a bright-coloured mound around the flag-pole. Rachel noticed Milly squatting there, wistfully fingering a silver star on the topmost coat.

Silly Milly, Rachel thought. They could have given her a badge. She's not a bother. Rachel took a rumpled star from her pocket and went over to her. "Here," she offered.

Milly looked thunderstruck and merely stared. "It's OK," soothed Rachel, pressing the star into her hand. "It's just a game." Milly grinned, then burst into a joyful dance around the playground, holding her star above her head, making it sparkle and fly. Rachel watched her and smiled.

But someone else suddenly noticed the happy dance and was not pleased. "Grab her!" commanded Lessie to Snapper. Milly was apprehended and held fast as Lessie began the interrogation.

"How dare you steal a star! Where did you get it? Tell me!" Milly burst into tears.

Rachel cringed for the helpless girl and clutched her stone. I should help her! But then Lessie would – Oh Miss B! I'm scared, really scared!

Lessie crumpled the star and threw it in the dirt. "It's got your dummy germs all over it. My mother says you should be in an—"

"Stop!" yelled Rachel. "Let her go. I gave her the star. It's only a stupid game. We were never ambassadors! It was only a game."

Lessie's eyes narrowed to tight little slits. Her jaw clenched and she folded her arms. "You mean it was a lie."

Milly sobbed. A crowd gathered.

Rachel felt her breath go out as if punched. "I didn't really lie – I was imagining. But you thought it was real – I didn't mean – I tried to tell you." Rachel's voice choked. "I'm sorry."

Lessie tore the star off her sweater. "Liar!" she shrieked as she threw the star at Rachel.

"*Liar! – Liar! – Liar!*" the crowd began to chant, as shiny stars began to rain around the trembling girl.

"What is going on! Stop this immediately!" Miss Brigham's arms encircled Rachel and Milly.

All was silent except for hiccuping sniffles. Then Lessie spoke. "Rachel lied. She wasn't an ambassador at all."

"My father says liars go to jail," added Snapper.

"That's enough!" ordered Miss Brigham. "You will line up and quietly return to class."

Miss Brigham knelt down beside the two girls. "I'm sorry this happened. I know everything seems really awful right now, but you'll see—"

Rachel saw Miss Brigham talking, but all she heard was the scream in her head — *Liar!liar!liar!liar!liar!liar!*

The teacher's words could not penetrate the echoing chant — I'll never have friends — I'll never have friends — I'll never, ever, ever have friends!

While they stood in line, Milly timidly took Rachel's hand and gave her a hesitant smile.

Leave me alone! thought Rachel wanting to shake away the thin fingers, push away the moments of shame. In a blur, she shuffled back to class. If only they wanted *me* — not some ambassadors' daughter. But now only Silly Milly will be my friend. Stupid! Stupid! Dumb!

Rachel stifled her tears, stared at her book and did not look up. I wish I could disappear. Maybe Daddy will quit his job or get transferred because he's such a success and we'll move far, far away where no one will ever know.

The rest of the day, Rachel held the stone in her pocket, imagining all the interesting places they could go. If only you were a magic wish stone. Courage is no good. It only makes everything worse.

I don't care, she thought, when the reading tests were handed back and she was in the slowest group. I don't care at all. But, when school was over, she felt her stomach tighten, waiting for the old green Chevy wagon to appear.

"What happened! What's wrong!" her mother exclaimed, the moment she saw Rachel's face.

"I'll tell you when we get home." Rachel ached with the need to throw herself into her mother's arms. She ached with wanting her father to magically appear and then – and then they'd all be together and drive and drive and never stop and she'd never have to explain.

Matthew, in his car bed, played with his Clownie and fussed and gurgled while their mother bit her lip and gripped the steering wheel.

At home, her mother nervously settled on the couch and began nursing Matthew. "Rachel, what's going on? Tell me exactly what happened. It can't be all that bad," she said with a pleading smile.

Rachel, trying not to cry, sat beside her mother and told the story.

Mrs Szeghetti's smile soon faded. "Rachel! To tell such a lie! To let people think—" She gasped. "Oh no! That's why those women were so very friendly. They thought – how will I explain?"

Seeing her mother upset, Rachel let loose her pent-up sobs. "I didn't mean to! Really! I didn't! I'm sorry, Mommy. I'm sorry!"

Matthew was startled and began to howl.

"Shhh," their mother whispered, gathering Rachel close and gently rocking her children, tears running down her cheeks. "I'm not mad. I know it's hard, always being someplace new, never fitting in, but it will get better. Shhhhh. It's OK. It's OK."

Slowly the sobs subsided. Rachel's face pressed against her mother's softness with its sweet-sour milky smell of baby. "Matthew's lucky. I wish I was still the baby and didn't go to school. I never want to go back there. Please let me stay home!"

Rachel's mother became very serious. "There will be no more running from problems. We've all done

45

that too much. Troubles don't go away, they just get bigger. You'll go to school tomorrow, hold your head up high and be proud of who you are – Rachel Szeghetti."

That night Rachel put the courage stone on the window ledge beside her bed. She whispered in the moonlight, "Courage doesn't feel very good. But maybe I didn't use you right or maybe you're still weak because I haven't used you enough – or maybe you're just a stupid stone." Hastily she pressed the stone to her cheek. "I'm sorry. I do believe in you. I do."

The next day there were lots of whispered comments and passed notes. Rachel knew they were all about her. At lunch time, Rachel shyly attempted to sit next to Donna and Susan. "Get lost!" said Donna and they stuck out their tongues and moved to another table. Milly smiled and eagerly started to come over, but Rachel frowned and turned away. I want to be by myself, she thought. I don't care if I don't have friends. I like being alone – that's what I'm used to.

Halfheartedly she opened her lunch box. All her favourite things were crammed inside. There was an apple with a carved smiling face, a cream cheese and olive sandwich with the crust cut off and three fresh-baked butterscotch chip cookies. Underneath the cookies was a note with stick figures of her mother, father, baby Matthew and Rachel. The note said: "Wherever we go, we will always be together. You are my wonderful girl. I love you very much. Keep smil-ing. Love, Mommy."

Chapter 6

HAUNTED

Hallowe'en was a week away and the children talked of nothing else but the annual Pennyville Carnival and costume contest. Rachel had still not chosen her costume. "I don't want to be a gypsy or a clown," Rachel replied to her mother's suggestions. "A boring costume won't win. I *need* to do something really special."

Mrs Szeghetti wearily looked up from the thick black ledger. "With Matthew teething and fussy, dinner to cook, and the house always a mess, I barely have time to do this bookkeeping. Your father's commission was less than we hoped – and we need the money. I don't have time."

"You don't understand! This is important!" I *need*

to win, thought Rachel. Then the other kids will think I'm special again.

"I wish you felt schoolwork was as crucial as making costumes and drawing all those pictures."

"Fine!" exclaimed Rachel. "I'll do it myself."

"That's not what I meant." Rachel's mother sighed. "I know this seems important to you and I'll help as soon as I'm done."

"Never mind," said Rachel, grabbing her jacket and slamming the door. All she cares about is Matthew and her stupid bookkeeping! Rachel grabbed a stick and threw it into the air. The sky was dirty grey as if the smoke from burning autumn leaves had formed one huge cloud. Rachel watched as a flock of crows approached from a distance. The black specks became flapping, cawing birds, circling around her head. They flew over the wall and vanished into the tall pines. Rachel felt for the stone in her pocket. Crows sure are a lot bigger than pigeons! Miss B talks to them. I wonder what else she does. I bet that big old house has lots of weird things inside. I bet Miss B would have all kinds of great spooky ideas for a costume! She helped me before, I bet she could help me again!

Rachel scraped her hand as she scaled the witch's wall. She wandered along the garden paths until she came to the two scowling, dragon-like creatures which guarded the entrance to the mansion. Rachel sucked the sting on her hand as she hurried past them. A lion's head knocker scowled down from the large front door. Rachel boldly rapped. There was no answer. Maybe witches get spookier around Hallowe'en. Maybe what Lessie said about her burning all those people – and the monster in the dungeon – maybe it's true! She rapped again, this time a little softer. No one's coming, she decided, almost with relief.

Suddenly, the door opened.

It's the lion knocker on the body of a giant! Rachel thought for a crazed instant. The looming face seemed more animal than human. One eyelid dripped into the cheek. The nose bulged purple, with small misshapen nostrils. Steel grey hair spun wild. The monster! It's the monster! Rachel gripped the stone in her pocket. I'm not going to run! I'm not going to run! Where's Miss B? Maybe he's escaped and killed her!

Behind the half-frozen monster face, a twisted smile emerged. His large hand reached out, holding a small yellowed piece of paper. Trembling, Rachel looked at the offered slip of paper and read – PLEASE COME IN. The monster bowed low, then with a sweep of his arm, motioned for Rachel to follow him into the dim, cavernous hall.

He doesn't *act* like he's going to eat me. I'm sure bad monsters are not so polite. I'll walk way behind him so he can't grab me and I'll just go in a little way and if I don't find Miss B – Wow! That chandelier looks like it's made of diamonds! I wonder who all those fancy people are in those big paintings? Maybe Miss B did meet kings and queens! Now curiosity led her through the dark rooms with their heavy curtains of velvet and brocade. They seemed to be peopled with motionless ghosts. I don't care if it's haunted. I'm not scared. As she rubbed her stone, she saw that the silent spirits were really furniture, lamps and pictures, covered in white sheets. Like a spook house, she told herself. Not scary at all. A smell of fresh baking began to penetrate the gloom. The giant thrust open a door on to a bright and cheery kitchen.

Miss B was regally seated at a table, about to slice a piece of brown bread. With her knife poised, she glared intently at Rachel. "I thought all that rap, rap, rapping might be you." She pointed the tip of her knife to a chair beside her. "Sit. Sam will take your jacket. I forgot, you haven't been formally introduced. Sam, this is Rachel, Rachel – Sam. He doesn't talk but his hearing is exceptional."

Sam bowed again. With his one good eye, Rachel thought she saw him wink. She attempted a shy smile, but the horror of his deformed face, now seen in light, made her smile seem more like a grimace.

"To be! To be! That is the question!" squawked a huge parrot perched on a metal stand. A tea kettle whistled, copper pots gleamed from the walls, and in a small raised fireplace, flames merrily danced. A large black and white cat leapt on to the counter.

"Will you have butter or marmalade?" asked Miss B, holding a thick steaming piece of bread.

Rachel stared at the parrot and said, "Butter, please."

"Butter, please! Butter, please!" squawked the parrot.

"Romeo! Mind your tongue! And, Figaro, get down from that counter." Miss B handed Rachel a piece of bread on a china plate. "What's the matter with your hand?"

"Nothing. I scraped it climbing over the wall."

"That's what comes from trespassing." Rachel flinched. "Well, no matter. What do you want this time? Did the courage stone work?"

"I have it right here." said Rachel. "It definitely works," she said glancing at Sam.

"And all the nonsense with that nasty little girl?"

Rachel wiggled uncomfortably. "I told the truth and everything, but it didn't feel so good."

"Comfort was not part of the guarantee." Miss B daintily wiped the corners of her mouth with her linen napkin.

"It was awful!" said Rachel. "Everybody got mad and no one will be my friend. Except Silly Milly and she's so dumb, Lessie's mom says she should be in an—" She stopped as Sam sat down at the table.

Miss B gazed intently at Rachel. "You were saying?"

Rachel swallowed. "Milly's OK. You said I can't 'make friends' I can only 'make myself'. But if I make a great costume and win the Hallowe'en contest, then maybe the other kids will want to be my friends too."

"Have some peppermint tea. It's from the garden. Sam, please. A cup for Rachel. I'm afraid you have not discerned my meaning. True friends aren't wooed by elaborate costumes. Costumes are mere covering." She gazed towards the ceiling, then, in a resonant voice she proclaimed, "Those drawn to the shimmer of stardom are blind as maggots to the light of the inner soul!"

51

Shyly, Rachel took the cup Sam offered and proceeded to plop five sugars into her tea. "But I really want friends."

"Have some marmalade. We made it with Spanish oranges."

"I only eat strawberry and grape."

"Have you ever tried orange marmalade?" Miss B pursed her lips and stared at Rachel. A lopsided grin contorted Sam's face as he passed the jar of marmalade to Rachel.

Reluctantly, Rachel dipped her knife into the orange goo and spread it thinly on her bread. Sweet orange and sour with a hint of flowers, the taste swelled in her mouth. "Yum!" Rachel glopped on more marmalade.

"Nothing ventured, nothing gained," replied Miss B.

"What is 'ventured'?"

"To attempt – to try. To dare the impossible."

"Like I'm going to have this incredible costume?"

Miss B sighed. "And what, may I ask, is this award-winning, friend-winning costume?"

"I'm not sure. I'm tired of being ugly," Rachel explained. "I want to be beautiful, but not boring like a princess or a fairy. I thought – maybe – you could do a magic spell."

"I have given you a courage stone. That is enough."

"I promise I'll never ask again!" pleaded Rachel.

"I doubt that is a promise you can keep!" snapped Miss B.

Rachel squeezed her napkin into a ball. "Maybe you're right. Sometimes I act pretty dumb. I just wanted to feel special. You know – not like me."

Miss B was silent a moment. When she spoke her voice was softer. "Yes. I do know. The desire for metamorphosis." She hesitated, then asked, "Have you thought of being a butterfly? A wire hanger could be bent for wings, then covered in pretty cloth."

"And I could draw butterfly designs! I'm a good artist! And maybe my mother would let me use the sequins she took off her old dress! It's a great idea!" Rachel exclaimed, nearly upsetting her tea. "I know I'll win!"

"At least you are not lacking in the essential ingredient of enthusiasm." Miss B sighed and sank against her chair. "I wish you well, but it is time for me to rest. All this chatter is quite wearing. Sam will show you to the door."

"I'll come back and show you my first prize ribbon!"

"Hmm. Yes. You do that."

In the garden, Rachel skipped and pranced past black-etched trees veining the powder-pink sky. "I will win! I will!"

Chapter 7
TORN

Rachel stared at herself in the long mirror on her parents' bedroom door. A magnificent orange, black and red butterfly stared back at her. Gold sequins twinkled along the outline of each wing.

Somehow her mother had found the time after all to sit with Rachel – special time, the two of them transforming sheets and wire and leotard into a glittering, magical butterfly. Close time, like before Matthew was born.

My costume is so beautiful, thought Rachel. I don't need magic to win the contest! Her father had seen her costume before he left on his selling trip. He had pronounced it the most amazing costume he had ever laid eyes on – a definite first prize. "And did you know?" he had said while adjusting his tie in the mirror. "The hall in the park where the contest is held? There was a jewel of a theatre in that very spot. An old guy in Canfield was telling me he used to go there when he was a boy. I asked what happened to it and he didn't want to tell me. Strange." Mr Szeghetti had kissed Rachel on the nose. "Now don't go flying away with those beautiful wings." She had grinned and pulled his moustache. Then he was gone. He said I would win first prize, Rachel remembered and touched her wing.

"Rachel!" called Mrs Szeghetti. "Are you sure a vest under your leotard will be warm enough?"

"I'm sure." Rachel slipped the smooth white courage stone into her black glove. "Let's go!"

Around the block from Rachel's house, directly across from the dark wooden gates leading to Miss B's, was a soaring arch of metal filigree spelling Dante's Park. In this grand and spacious place of brick paths, rolling lawns and gracious trees, cast-iron animals peered from behind bushes and old-fashioned lamp-posts drooped like giant wilted flowers. A cobbled road went through the centre of the park and led to the library and auditorium where the annual Hallowe'en Festival was in full swing.

"Goodness!" exclaimed her mother, carrying Matthew. "I didn't realize there'd be so many people."

Costumed children crowded along the walkways. The path was lit with glowing jack-o'-lanterns and a real skeleton dangled next to the auditorium door. In the bustling hall, they were greeted with smells of popcorn and fresh-fried doughnuts. Matthew immediately began to cry at the blaring noise.

"Oh, dear! Rachel, sweetie. Here's a dollar. Why don't you buy some doughnuts and look around? I'll wait outside and come in when they do the parade. Then it won't be so loud." Reluctantly, Rachel took the money and watched her mother hustle away. She always wants me to make friends, thought Rachel. But she's so shy, she never makes friends either!

Her wings bumped against people in the crowd. She mumbled, "Sorry," and stumbled towards a group of classmates waiting for the next batch of doughnuts. Rachel stood to one side wishing her hair, pulled in a bun, wasn't so obviously red. Susan, in a witch costume was talking to Donna, who was dressed as a princess with printed ruffles and bows.

"Yoo-hoo! Girls!" called a familiar voice. "I'm glad I found you." Emerging from the crowd was a pink satin gown with lace ruffles, crystal buttons and sleeves puffed at the shoulders. Atop blonde, banana curls, sat a rhinestone tiara. There was a stunned silence as Lessie walked towards her friends holding a white, rabbit fur cape.

Rachel, the glorious butterfly, felt herself shrinking into a drab, lowly caterpillar as she compared her costume to Lessie's.

Donna fingered the elastic of her own inexpensive mask, as she cooed her compliments. "Lessie, you look beautiful."

"My mother had her dressmaker sew it. Did you see my silver slippers?" Out from the billows of pink, Lessie pointed a silver toe.

"Are those really diamonds on your head?" asked Donna.

Lessie gave her a benevolent smile. "Maybe," she replied. "Susan, weren't you a witch last year?" Rachel shuffled behind a tall vampire, grateful to be hidden from Lessie's sneer. Adjusting her crown, Lessie continued. "Well, at least you aren't a cat. Silly Milly is dancing around going 'Miaow! Miaow! Miaow!' What a dummy!" Lessie rolled her eyes and the girls laughed. "Oh, no! Here she comes!"

Milly held her black tail, dancing, smiling and sweetly mewing. Rachel felt a twinge of protective panic as she approached.

"Oh, Silly Milly!" Lessie called. "Come here and show us your costume." Milly gaily bounced over. "What a good monkey you are." Lessie smirked for the benefit of her admiring comrades.

"I'm a cat!" Milly replied proudly.

"You can't be a cat!" exclaimed Lessie, shaking her head.

Milly looked puzzled.

"No." Lessie grabbed Milly's tail. "This is a monkey tail," she said, in a mock serious tone. She touched Milly's nose. "This is a monkey face." She sniffed. "And this is a monkey smell! Phew!!" Donna and Susan burst into gales of laughter. Milly's head drooped.

Rachel clenched the stone within her glove and imagined grabbing Lessie's crown and stomping it into tiny pieces. She imagined tearing Lessie's costume off and ripping it to shreds. Instead, she stepped forward and grabbed Milly's arm. "You can be a cat if you want to," she declared, reminding herself of Miss B's commanding voice. "Come on." As she pulled on

Milly's arm, Lessie held firm to Milly's tail. "RRIIIIIP! went the costume.

Lessie grinned. "See what you did? You ripped her costume. Here." She tossed Rachel the tail. "Oh, Rachel. Your coat hanger's showing."

Laughter erupted and Rachel's face burned. She pushed Milly through the crowd, away from the jeering girls. Tears smeared the painted whiskers.

"Don't cry. I'll fix your tail," Rachel reassured. They hurried into the clear autumn air. "My mom has pins for nappies," Rachel explained, dragging Milly along. "You'll see."

Her mother looked so peaceful sitting on the bench, leaning against the tree, holding the sleeping Matthew. Rachel wanted to curl into her lap and cry. Instead, she showed her the torn costume and asked if they could borrow some pins. Mrs Szeghetti said hello to Milly and told Rachel to rummage through her bag. With one arm free from Matthew, she helped Rachel pin Milly's tail. "We had better go inside, I think I hear the parade."

"I'm not going," said Rachel.

"But, Rachel! It's all you've talked about for weeks."

"I don't care. I'm not going."

Milly touched Rachel's wing. "Pretty butterfly."

Rachel shook her wing away. "It is not."

"What happened in there?" asked her mother.

"Stupid kids! I don't want to go, that's all."

Milly pried open Rachel's tight fist. She clasped Rachel's hand and with her smeared, grinning face, she said sweetly, "Miaow."

Rachel sighed. "Miaow," she replied, feeling the hard stone beneath her glove. Over her tongue, rolled the sweet memory of marmalade. *Nothing ventured, nothing gained.* It's no use, thought Rachel. *Dare the impossible!* I can't, Rachel replied to the voice within her.

"Well, I want to see the parade," Mrs Szeghetti announced.

Milly tugged slightly on Rachel's hand.

Courage, Miss B had said. *It increases every time you use it.* Rachel sighed. "OK, OK. I'll come," she muttered.

As the line formed, each person was handed a number. Lessie and her court were way up front. Marching music came from a scratchy record and the parade began circling around the auditorium. Milly's parents spotted her and waved. Rachel lost sight of her mother. After the parade, each person went on stage and took a bow in front of the judges. The crowd oohed and aahed as Lessie, rhinestones twinkling, entered the spotlight and curtsied.

Milly bounced with excitement as she and Rachel moved along the line. But when it was her turn, Milly froze and refused to budge. The officials began to motion for her to hurry. The crowd began to murmur.

"I'll go with you," Rachel whispered.

The cat and butterfly climbed the stairs and bowed. The crowd clapped politely. Milly ran off the stage to her parents. Rachel's mother, holding sleeping Matthew, found Rachel and gave her a one-armed squeeze. They bought doughnuts and cider

59

and waited for the winners to be announced.

"That was sweet what you did for that nice little girl," said her mother. "You're the most beautiful butterfly *I've* ever seen. We had fun together, making the costume, didn't we?"

"Yeah," agreed Rachel. "Like before."

A voice calling numbers blared over the loud-speaker. The first category was "most beautiful". Rachel felt her stone and wished hard – but Lessie won. The pink princess sparkled as she came on stage and accepted her ribbon. The butterfly didn't win second, third or even honorable mention.

Trembling, Rachel pulled her mother towards the door. "Let's go."

As they were leaving, her mother turned. "Rachel! They're calling your number!" Excitedly, Rachel hurried to the stage and up the stairs where the judge asked her name.

"Rachel Szeghetti!" he announced. "Honorable mention for most unusual!" The crowd clapped, but Rachel's classmates were busy surrounding Lessie and didn't notice.

"Congratulations!" exclaimed her mother.

Rachel frowned and stuffed the ribbon into her glove. "Butterflies are beautiful, not 'unusual'!"

That night, Rachel placed the ribbon next to her stone in the underwear drawer. "Unusual" means "different" or "weird". Silly Milly is different and weird. I don't want to be like her. I want to be like the rest of the kids. She lay curled in a tight ball beneath the covers.

Stripy jumped on her bed and snuggled close on her pillow. No I don't, she thought. I don't want to be like anybody. I just want to be alone. I don't want to even see Miss B. I told her I was going to win and I didn't. Down the hall, she could hear the faint cry of Matthew and then the opening of doors as her mother hurried to him. "I hate it here, I hate everything," she moaned and fell asleep, buried in the sound of Stripy's purr.

Chapter 8
DARKNESS

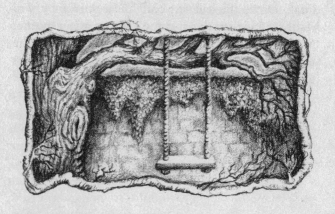

"Where do monsters come from?" Rachel asked her father as he checked the thick rope he'd knotted around the oak tree's lowest branch.

"Well, Frankenstein's monster came from dead bodies. Long ago there was this mad scientist and he—"

"No! I mean *real* monsters."

"Like the kind that hide under your bed?"

"You promised not to tease me about that any more. Is the swing ready? Can I sit on it?"

"Take it away!"

Rachel positioned herself on the centre of the wooden seat and her father gave her a big push. "Why are you asking about monsters?" he asked. "Met any good ones lately?"

Rachel bit her lip. She thought about Sam and Miss B all the time, but had not been to visit. She was ashamed to admit she hadn't won either the prize or the acceptance from the class. How could she have imagined her problems would all be solved by winning a dumb contest? Besides, Rachel was beginning to feel funny not telling her parents about her journeys over the wall. She was used to keeping secrets, but there were so many questions she wanted to ask. Maybe there was a reason why everyone in town seemed to hate Miss B. Maybe she did do something really bad. But then wouldn't she be in jail? It was hard imagining Miss B behind bars. And what about Sam?

Rachel and her mother had gone to the garden shop to inquire about the cost of sowing grass seed in the spring. The man's face had lit up when he heard where they lived. "How's the garden doing?" he had asked. "Can you see it from your house? I used to go there with my father. He was friends with the gardener before—" The man had stopped abruptly and had suddenly become very busy watering the plants. "Come back in April," he had said.

Rachel had wanted to ask, "Was that Sam? Do you know him?" But then her mother would have wanted an explanation and gotten all upset when she had the reply. It was easier to stay in her room, hug her cat and draw pictures. No questions, no problems. No one to worry, no way to get hurt. Safe. I like being alone, she concluded.

"Monster got your tongue?" her father asked, giving her a push.

"Rachel!" called her mother, standing on the back porch. "Why aren't you wearing gloves and a hat? It's ridiculous putting a swing up in mid-November, Alfred. It's too cold. She'll get sick."

"She'll be fine. My girl wants a swing, she gets a swing," replied Mr Szeghetti, going over and giving his wife a hug. "You want to try?"

"Heaven's no! I'm way behind on the ledger due this week and I haven't even started dinner. Mattie must be cutting six teeth, the way he's been fussing. Besides, it's almost dark."

"Just a few minutes more, Mommy. Please?"

"Oh, all right," agreed Mrs Szeghetti. "But then come right in!"

Rachel swung higher and higher, watching the lights come on one by one as darkness swept around her. Her hands were frozen and her ears felt like ice. But she didn't care.

A few days later, Matthew was the one who got sick. A running nose went to fever then flu, hovering on the edge of pneumonia. Every night he coughed and cried. Rachel could hear her mother going back and forth bringing cool face cloths and medicine. The days passed and Rachel saw her mother's face become like a clenched fist, gripping the worry, holding it fast.

"Mom. Can you put my hair in braids?" Rachel asked one morning.

"Not now," replied Mrs Szeghetti, looking past Rachel, listening for Matthew's cry. "You'll have to walk to school again. The doctor is still concerned about Mattie's lungs, so I can't drive you."

"I don't mind," said Rachel.

But she did. The long trek to school gave her plenty of time to wallow in misery and list all her woes. Mommy doesn't even know I'm here. She never asks, "How was school?" She hasn't helped me with my homework since Matthew got sick. Rachel remembered the doctor's serious face as he listened to Matthew's tiny chest. What if Matthew died? It would be sad, but then maybe her father would quit the job that kept him away from home and they'd move to some new place and be together again, just the three of them. Rachel heard the school bell and began to run. Oh, well, she thought. One more late slip to add to my collection.

Rachel was spending more and more time in her room with the door closed and her feelings locked. "I don't care if I'm dumb," she told Stripy. "School is stupid. Everything's stupid." She remembered the disappointed, pitying look on Miss Brigham's face when she had handed back the test. Rachel crossed her arms, her shoulders drawn up near her ears. "What difference will it make if I study? They still won't like me."

One morning, Mrs Szeghetti found a mouldy sandwich on Rachel's dresser nestled between some dirty socks and crumpled paper. There was a glass with a few inches of sour milk left on the windowsill.

"This place is a disgrace!" her mother proclaimed. "And your marbles are all over the floor. If Matthew crawled in here and put one in his mouth, he could die! Can't you take any responsibility?"

"My room's not so bad," replied Rachel, silently kicking a half-eaten apple under her bed.

"Clean it up now!" ordered Mrs Szeghetti, marching downstairs.

When is Mom going to stop being so cross? thought Rachel as she stuffed her crumpled clothes in a drawer. Matthew was better, but he was still weak and had lost a lot of weight. Her mother always seemed to be holding him with his Clownie or fixing him something to eat.

"Nothing is the same any more!" Rachel told Stripy who was energetically biting at a flea. "I remember when the month before Christmas was so exciting, I thought I was going to bust! Maybe that's what happens when you get older – all the magic goes away."

Throwing her shoes in the wardrobe and retrieving a sweater from the floor, Rachel found the forgotten old newspapers pushed in the corner. I'll copy drawings, she decided, spreading the frail yellow pages across her bed. She stared when she saw a picture of a beautiful woman in a fancy gown. On her shoulder was a parrot. Below the picture was a caption and an article: Local heroine, Beatrice Baumgartner, returns from France after a successful season as the star of Paris theatre.

Rachel studied the drawing. The parrot looks a lot like Romeo, but then I guess all parrots look pretty much the same. 1897 was – let me see, this is 1959 . . . She scribbled on a piece of paper. Sixty-two years ago!

Rachel read the whole article, sounding out the

long words as best she could. That's what I want to do when I grow up! Travel everywhere and have lots of adventures – instead of being stuck in this dumpy place. She returned the pages to the closet. Somehow drawing pictures seemed like a boring thing to do and only made her feel more lonely.

Outside, the day was grey and cold. The mansion's turrets rose up beyond the mesh of leafless limbs. Rachel could see smoke coming from one of the tall chimneys. Miss B and Sam are sitting beside the fire, drinking tea, she thought. The memory of fresh bread seemed to rise inside her. Sharp hunger awakened the loneliness she had tried to forget. The pang ripped through the cocoon she had spun around herself. Being alone was not what she wanted any more. It hurt too much.

She began to rummage through her drawers. Where's my stone? She found it and slipped the smooth white rock into her pocket, put on her jacket, tip-toed downstairs and ran outside.

The air was bitter, the ground still snowless. She stamped on the fragile ice of a frozen puddle, satisfied to shatter the winter quiet. "So there!" she said to the world, kicking the thin shards. With numb fingers Rachel scaled the wall. Grass crunched beneath her feet and branches snapped as she ran past the brittle arms of trees.

Sam answered the door. Rachel chewed on her braid, tried not to stare at his ugly features smeared about his face. She took his offered hand and said a faint hello. The empty rooms rang with cold. Not until they opened the door to the kitchen did Rachel fully remember the warmth she had missed, the feeling of magic. Miss B was seated by the fire, stroking Figaro, the cat.

"Parley-voo français?" squawked Romeo.

He does look like the parrot in the picture, thought Rachel.

"My dear, come sit by the fire," Miss B commanded, tapping the footstool with her cane. "You look chilled to the bone. What mischief have you been up to these days? We were expecting a visit from a beautiful butterfly."

"I didn't win."

"I see."

Sam brought a bowl of soup, a linen napkin and two hot buttered biscuits. "Thank you," Rachel said, holding the bowl of soup, feeling the steam against her face. "It's delicious. My mother used to make soup, before Matthew was born." Images floated by of her family together, cosy and happy like they used to be. But those times were gone. A thawed bit of sadness slid down her cheek.

"I will not press you to discuss private matters," said Miss B, handing her a clean handkerchief. "But lending handkerchiefs is becoming a habit."

Rachel swallowed the biscuit past the lump in her throat. "Everything's awful. No one wants to be my friend. My father is never home, and my mother loves Matthew now, not me!" Rachel cried, trying not to choke.

Miss B patted Rachel's hand. "I have not much experience with babies. However, I am certain that a feeble infant cannot possibly compete with a bright young girl who wants to please her parents. Have you been working on your Christmas presents?"

Rachel shook her head.

"Well, there you go. Nothing makes a person crankier than approaching a moment of giving empty-handed. I know the perfect gift for a child your age to give her parents. Do they have any handkerchiefs embroidered by you?"

"No, but—"

"The word 'but' is filled with failure. Erase it from your vocabulary. Sam, would you be so kind as to bring me my sewing basket?"

"I don't know how to embroider," Rachel timidly explained. "I've only sewn popcorn for the Christmas tree."

Miss B scowled as if Rachel were messenger of terrible news. "I suspected the world was hell-bent on ruin, but this is ridiculous. What do they teach young girls?"

Rachel pinched a biscuit crumb and felt embarrassed.

"Well, it's high time you learned something useful."

Between sips of hot, spiced cider, Rachel learned to tighten the hoop, design a pattern and sew elementary stitches. They also cut out corduroy in the shape of a bunny to stuff as a present for Matthew.

"Miss B," Rachel asked, as she embroidered the bunny's eye. "Do the crows understand when you talk to them?"

"We have had generations of practice. The ancestors of those same crows were a terrible torment to me as a child. They would pull my hair ribbons, steal my toys and tell my mother all my secrets. Quite annoying."

Rachel hesitated. "Why do I have to keep you secret?"

"Your thread is short, time to knot. People have their reasons. I will not be talked about behind my back."

That's what's strange, thought Rachel. Everyone drops hints but no one talks about *what* happened. Maybe I don't want to know. Maybe it's better not to ask. Rachel sighed. Besides, no one is my friend enough to tell.

"Not so tight," snapped Miss B. "You'll pull the material."

"Don't you ever get lonely? Sometimes I see the kids playing together and I get this feeling inside like a big dark wind. I think if only I were more like them, maybe they'd like me and I wouldn't be alone."

"Loneliness is a state of mind. My life, in the company of Sam, is richer and more varied than people with a thousand friends. That stitch is sloppy. Pull it out."

"I wish I could be just like you!"

"My life does not lend itself to reproduction."

"Have you always lived in Pennyville?"

"Do you think that anyone with the smallest degree of sophistication could have 'always lived in Pennyville'? I have travelled so far and wide for so many years, memories alone can sustain me. Knot the end of your stitches. It is late and time you were returning home."

Rachel sighed as she buttoned her coat. "Everything is so dreary out. I wish there was magical snow that could cover everything in my life and make it new!"

"You are always trying to cover things over – costumes, snow! Covering problems doesn't solve them," replied Miss B. "Underneath the snow the dreariness remains."

Sam tapped Miss B on the shoulder and made motions with his hands. Miss B smiled. "Sam, as usual, you are correct. He said, under the snow your mouse-tulip is beginning to grow. Transformations. Snow covers and time changes." Sam looked directly at Rachel and made more motions with his hands. Miss B explained. "He says you did well with the embroidery – and I endorse that sentiment."

Rachel gave him the first real smile. "Thank you. And thank you, Miss B, for the handkerchiefs and stuff. I'll come back soon."

"Before you go." Miss B fumbled in the pocket of her dress. "It is neither safe nor proper for you to be climbing over that high wall. However, entering by the front gate is sure to arouse questions." She handed Rachel a long black key. "This is to the back garden door. I must be turning into an addle-brained old woman, giving my key to a pert-nosed, pig-tailed little girl. Well – no matter."

"Oh, Miss B! Thank you! Thank you! Thank you!"

"One thank you is quite sufficient. I am trusting that you are a reasonably responsible little girl and will keep my key safe?"

"I wouldn't dream of losing it!"

Miss B cocked one eyebrow. "I've found that

dreaming and doing are often entirely different."

"I'll keep it next to the stone you gave. My two favourite things!"

"Yes. Well." Miss B looked over at Sam who was stroking the cat. "You needn't look so smug." She turned back to Rachel and said gruffly, "And it's time for *you* to scurry on home."

It was almost supper time when Rachel sneaked up the stairs and hid the sewing bag. "I'm going to make my parents wonderful presents and never do anything bad ever again. I'll be so good Mommy won't have anything to be cross about." She bounced downstairs into the kitchen. Her mother was scraping burned carrots from the pot. Rachel put her arms around her mother. "I'll be good and keep my room clean – I promise!"

"It's OK," replied her mother, patting Rachel's back. "Set the table, please. Your father's not getting home until late, so we'll go ahead and eat."

At dinner, Rachel picked at her piece of fish. Mommy never even knew I was gone, she thought. She looked across the table and saw the deep circles around her mother's eyes. Mom's tired, and always so busy, I wonder if *she* ever gets lonely? I know she misses Daddy. I'll try harder to be good.

Mother and daughter washed the dishes and made the kitchen neat and tidy, but as they turned out the light, Rachel noticed the smell of burned carrots still remained. Sometimes it's hard to make things go away, she thought.

Chapter 9

COLD

"I want you all to explore the world of written matter!" exclaimed Miss Brigham. "See how exciting reading can be." Miss Brigham had decorated the room for Christmas. Green and red loops hung from the ceiling and large paper candy canes were tacked on the bulletin board. The stripes were to be filled in with the names of books, magazines or articles read. The students were supposed to fill their candy canes by Christmas vacation.

Rachel's candy cane was empty and Christmas was only three weeks away. *I wonder if I can use newspaper articles that are almost eighty years old? Even the kids in my group have read something.* The slowest reading group was also the smallest.

"Silly Milly sounds like she's going to throw up

when she reads," declared Snapper, throwing an airplane to Billy Boudreau.

"Snapper!" Miss Brigham rebuked. "You will keep your negative comments and name-calling to yourself!"

But it's true! Rachel inwardly agreed. Milly tries too hard and her throat gets tight and her face turns red. Rachel always made sure she appeared bored and unconcerned when it was her turn to read.

"You four are making good progress," said Miss Brigham. "Now put your books away. Time for lunch."

In the cafeteria, Rachel sat alone in her usual spot making doodles on her paper napkin. She watched as Lessie and her gang encircled Milly.

"That's a dummy, I mean yummy sandwich," Lessie cooed. "Can I have a bite?"

Trusting, Milly offered Lessie her sandwich.

"Oh!" exclaimed Lessie. "I forgot! I'm allergic to turkey turds." Several of the girls twittered.

Rachel chomped on her apple. Milly is so stupid! She lets them make fun of her! She glanced and saw Milly's usually happy face, full of loneliness and hurt. I don't care, Rachel told herself, hungrily eating her cookie. It's her own fault!

On the playground, icy swing chains and metal climbing bars froze fingers and pulled skin. Lessie and her girls huddled by the storage shed, hiding from the biting wind. Rachel, hands in pockets, wandered, dreaming. And Milly danced. Spinning in her world of solo rapture, she leapt gracefully around the frozen yard.

She's almost pretty, thought Rachel, observing with envy Milly's joyous, unselfconscious movement. The dancing trance led to a remote area of the field. Rachel followed. Milly noticed Rachel and beckoned with her smile. Hesitant, cautious, Rachel slowly moved. Then, releasing, she lifted her arms, flinging herself to internal songs. Around and around they danced, silent, unspeaking, oblivious to cold.

The next day, the principal announced winter was truly here, and recess would be held in the gym. Lessie and Donna and Susan all took ballet and were constantly chattering about the Christmas recital. Rachel had asked her mother if she could have lessons, but her mother said it was too expensive, so Rachel just drew ballerinas in the margins of her books and imagined the fairy costumes and sets. Now in the gym, Lessie decided to impart her knowledge of ballet and drill the girls on the *plié arabesque*. Rachel stayed close, hungry to be included.

"Hey! Spaghetti head!" called Lessie. "Want to be a ballerina? I could show you how."

Rachel nodded. Maybe Lessie saw me dancing yesterday and thought I was good enough to be a ballerina.

All the girls watched intently as Lessie walked over to Rachel. "Ballet has a lot of rules you'd have to follow. Understand?"

"I will," agreed Rachel. "I'll follow the rules."

Lessie squinted her eyes. "Are you sure?"

"Oh, yes!" said Rachel, nodding vigorously.

"We saw you yesterday with Silly Milly—"

That's it! thought Rachel. They saw we could dance!

"We don't want *her* hanging around," continued Lessie. "So if you want to be with us, you have to tell Silly Milly to get lost. You have to be really mean or she won't listen. Agreed?"

"But," said Rachel. "Maybe if I just explained—"

"*No!*" Lessie snapped. "You have to say something nasty and we have to hear it! Unless – you'd rather dance with *her.*"

"Come on, Rachel," Donna coaxed. "Silly Milly is used to having people say things like that to her. She doesn't care."

Rachel breathed deep, ready to leap the abyss separating her from the promised acceptance. I want to be like the other girls. I'm tired of being unusual. I want to fit in.

"Hey Silly Milly!" Rachel called. Milly came bounding over like a friendly puppy. "I think your kind of dancing is dumb."

"Say more!" whispered Lessie.

"You're dirty and disgusting and I don't want your germs!"

Milly stared, stunned at this new voice of attack. Her mouth hung open, her eyes were luminous and large.

Go away! thought Rachel. Leave me alone! Don't look at me like that! I *had* to do it! "Get out of here!" she said.

"Yeah," said Lessie, sidling next to Rachel. "Get out of here!"

Rachel had done it. She was included. She was one of them.

Now every day at recess Rachel lined up between Donna and Susan and submitted to Lessie's barrage of orders and criticisms. "Two *pliés* in second position! Stand up straight! Point your toes!" Rachel was allowed to sit at their table at lunch, but they still whispered things so she wouldn't hear. A lot of conversation centred around colours of nail polish and deciding who was the jerkiest person they had ever seen. When they teased Milly or some of the kids in the younger grades, Rachel felt embarrassed and kept silent. She was glad it was almost Christmas vacation.

The handkerchiefs were done. She had used her allowance and bought two more, one for Miss B and one for Sam. Every day Rachel had looked forward to escaping Lessie and doing something all on her own. Many of the stitches were crooked, and the bunny had one ear higher than the other, but she knew everyone would like their hand-made, hand-stitched presents.

Soon it was late in the afternoon of Christmas Eve. The presents for Miss B and Sam were neatly wrapped and hidden along with the key in the pocket of her coat. The day sped by and still they remained undelivered. Rachel's father sat on the floor struggling with the Christmas tree lights.

"Darn it! Meg, I'm going down to the hardware and pick up some replacement bulbs." He threw the bulbs on the couch. "I'll be back in a jiffy."

"Popcorn! Popcorn! Who wants popcorn!" Rachel's mother sang, entering from the kitchen with a big bowl.

"I do! I do!" Rachel sang back.

Mrs Szeghetti's eyes were shining as she set the bowl beside Rachel. "Doesn't the house look pretty with evergreens above the windows and such a big tree? We're having a genuine old-fashioned Christmas. Don't eat all the popcorn. A real Christmas tree must have at least one long strand."

Rachel, with her new sewing skills, strung the popcorn faster than ever before, cracking only a few. The fireplace and greens were nice. Now if only it would snow. Then everything would look perfect.

"What a good job you're doing," said Rachel's mother, returning with Matthew. "I'm finally baking those cookies I've been trying to make all week. I thought I was never going to get all that bookkeeping done! Will you watch Mattie? He can play on the floor with Clownie."

"Sure," replied Rachel, knotting the end of a strand.

Matthew hugged Clownie, and chewed on the soft cloth hand. Rachel threw a piece of popcorn in the air and caught it with her mouth. Tossing, giggling, she continued, some landing in her mouth, some not. I'd better clean this mess, she thought, crawling around, hunting for stray kernels.

Then Matthew made a funny sound. Rachel saw him standing, clutching the couch, tree lights in his hand.

"Matthew!" Rachel yelled, trying to pry away the lights. "Let go!" Matthew kept his mouth tightly closed.

Rachel's mother came rushing in with floury white hands. "Oh! No! Matthew! What do you have in your mouth?" Reaching inside, she removed two red glass bulbs. "He could have died!" Her voice quivered. "If the glass had broken and he had swallowed—"

"It's not my fault! Daddy put the lights there!"

"But I told you to watch him." Rachel's mother clutched Matthew to her and rocked him back and forth.

Rachel gingerly picked up Clownie to give to her baby brother. "I'm sorry, Mommy."

"I can't trust you," snapped her mother.

Rachel, wounded, cried back: "I said I was sorry!"

She flung on her coat and fled out into the deepening dusk, Clownie still in her hand. It's all Matthew's fault! I hate him! I wish he'd never been born. I wish he would die! Rachel stared with hatred at the limp clown and his persistent grin. She shook him so violently his head ripped at the neck. "Stupid clown!" She heaved him into the bushes and ran to the place where all seemed ordered and nothing impossible. With tears and rage, Rachel inserted the key and kicked the back wall door until finally the lock released its rusty hold. She entered the darkening garden.

She imagined Matthew choking on the glass and slowly dying as her parents helplessly stood by. She imagined his body, lifeless like her mouse-tulip. A whoosh of wings, glimpse of black, flew through the shadowy sky. Rachel paused at the bottom of the steps. Even Miss B wouldn't like me if she knew I was so bad and horrible. If Matthew died, he would never grow up or talk or play kids' games. He'd never know magic – or Santa Claus!

Rachel took the packages from her pocket and laid them by the door. She turned and wandered around the drab and dormant grounds until she found the cherub on the bird bath, still smiling, untouched by freezing weather. Rachel knelt in front of the tiny grave.

"Oh, Mouse-tulip! I don't really want my brother to be dead and lying under the ground. I know I'm stupid and dumb and lots of times bad. I didn't like being so awful to Milly. Sometimes I feel so dark and mad inside – meanness just comes out. But I think I used to be good, when I was little. Please, Mouse-tulip, make me the old Rachel. Make me the Rachel my mommy loved."

Her teeth began to chatter as winter seeped into her knees. "I'll find his clown and bring it back. I promise. Goodbye, Mouse-tulip." Rachel stood and touched the plump-winged baby. "Merry Christmas."

She searched and searched the bushes, but could not find the broken clown. "Why can't I find Clownie? Why?"

The pale blind eye of the rising moon stared out above the trees. "Caw! Caw!" sang several crows. One seemed to be carrying something in its beak.

"Talking crows and courage stones and a Mouse-tulip – maybe none of it's real. Real is Clownie gone,

80

and me – bad. There is no such thing as magic." Slowly Rachel dragged home.

Mrs Szeghetti had on her coat and was coming to find her daughter. "I was worried. Mattie's fine. I'm sorry I yelled. Let's trim the tree and have a Merry Christmas."

"Try a cookie," her father suggested. "Best ones I've ever tasted, and I'm regarded as an expert when it comes to cookies!"

Rachel took a cookie and slowly munched. It could have been cardboard for all she cared. Carefully she hung ornaments on prickly boughs, breathed the spicy smell of pine and tried to fill herself with Christmas spirit. But all she could see was Matthew without his favourite clown. They haven't missed Clownie – not yet. They'll think it's just misplaced – like sometimes happens. But then they'll search and Mattie will cry, and then . . . The thought of having to tell was too horrible.

"I'm not hungry," she explained at supper, then brought down her presents, all carefully wrapped in sparkly tissue and tied with neat red bows.

Mrs Szeghetti surveyed the room with its candles and pine boughs and sprigs of holly. "Isn't it wonderful to have a real fireplace and mantel to hang the stockings! I always dreamed of being in a house like this! This old house was meant for Christmas." She tidied the cookies on the plate for Santa and neatly arranged the carrots for his reindeer. "Are you OK?" she asked Rachel who was twisting a bit of tinsel.

"I'm fine, just tired," Rachel answered.

Mr Szeghetti tucked Rachel in bed and kissed her

forehead for "sugar-plum dreams". In the dark, her mother sat by her pillow and sang *Silent Night*. At the words "mother and child", Rachel longed to cry and fling herself into her mother's arms, but instead she hugged her pillow. She couldn't explain what she had done. It was too awful.

Chapter 10
SNOWFALL

Rachel awoke. Silhouettes of white-dusted branches emerged in the pale morning sky. *Christmas!* was Rachel's first thought, then – *Snow!* But soon other thoughts darkened her awakening jubilation. *Matthew will cry and they'll look for Clownie. Then they'll find out how bad I am.*

She lay, watching colours return to the room. *I could say I don't know where it went. They'd never know. Liar-liar-liar-liar* came the chant. She remembered the rain of falling stars, Milly's look of hurt. *It isn't true what I said about Milly. She isn't dirty. I lied so they'd be my friends, but they're not really my friends – and now I don't like myself.*

Stripy jumped on the bed and lay purring on her chest. "You just like me 'cause you don't know better.

You wouldn't like me if you knew." Rachel wiped her tears on Stripy's fur. "Miss B told me the only friend I could make was myself – and I'm not doing a very good job."

She heard Miss B's voice: *Only one exit from the maze of lies!* If only – no. I just have to face it, that's all. Rachel hugged her cat. She slipped on robe and slippers, put the courage stone in her pocket and crept down the hall.

Her parents' room smelled of sleep. Rachel touched her mother's shoulder. Her mother, crawling from dreams, murmured, "Merry Christmas."

"Mommy," Rachel whispered, rubbing on the courage stone. "I did something terrible and I want to tell you and get all the angry stuff over before it's time for Christmas."

Mrs Szeghetti pushed half way up to sitting. "What are you talking about?"

"Clownie's gone!" Rachel's voice grew louder as she cried, "I ripped him and threw him in the bushes. Then I felt sorry and looked and looked – but he was lost. Oh Mommy! I didn't mean to be so bad!"

Rachel's father groaned and opened half an eye. "What's all this ruckus? Sounds like a train coming through the room!"

"Ssshhh, Alfred. This is serious. Rachel is upset." She lifted the covers and pulled Rachel in. "You're not bad," soothed her mother. "You just make mistakes."

"But, Mommy, I was mean to Milly 'cause I didn't want the kids thinking I was weird like her. And I hated Matthew because everything changed when he was born and I feel like you love him, not me. But I know why you're always mad – it's because I'm so bad."

"I'm sorry you were mean to Milly," said her mother. "But now you can be nice. And Matthew will love something else besides Clownie. It's only a toy clown. You are my good, dear daughter. I love you very much and always will, no matter what you do."

"But, Mommy," Rachel began, her voice cracking with the sobs locked in her throat. "I wanted Matthew to die!"

Rachel's mother curled her warmth around her daughter and held her close. "I'm sure you did, but he didn't die and you both will grow and you will be his sister. We all get angry. We all make mistakes." The familiar smell of her mother's old blue nightgown felt soggy, warm and safe.

"Yeah," agreed her father. "I shouldn't have left the light bulbs on the couch."

"And I shouldn't have yelled," continued her mother. "I was scared and took it out on you. I've been tense and yelling a lot lately – I'm sorry."

"Sure is a lot of gabbing and tears for Christmas morning," said Mr Szeghetti, twirling his moustache. "Did I ever tell you about the time I got coal for Christmas?"

Rachel shook her head and snuffed back some straggling tears. Her mother stroked her hair.

"Now that was something to cry about!" said her father. "I woke up real early Christmas morning and was going to sneak into the living room and see my

85

presents. But when I opened the door to my bedroom, I found a bucket of coal hanging on the door knob! I had not been what you would call a perfect child, so I knew that Santa had decided that was all I was worth. My humiliation was so great, I decided to hide the evidence outside. Climbing out of my bedroom window on to a neighbouring tree was something I had done before, but never in winter, and never in my pyjamas and bare feet. The branches were icy and the ground covered in snow. Then to add to my predicament, the window slammed shut. They found me about a half hour later, up in the tree, shivering and howling, holding my bucket of coal."

"So what happened?"

"My father got a ladder and helped me down."

"And then?"

"I went inside and put on warm clothes."

"But the coal! Did you get any other presents?"

"As a matter of fact I did. I got an electric train – with two coal cars! That bucket came in very handy."

Rachel smiled. "So you really hadn't been *that* bad. I mean they still loved you and forgave you and all that stuff."

"Yeah," agreed her father. "All that good stuff. My parents loved me and I love you. I wish I was around to tell you more. I miss you and Mattie and your mom so much! But sometimes we have to do things that are hard and not a lot of fun. If I'm a success, I'll be able to travel less. The company always gives the new guy the worst routes. That's just the way it is."

"But why do you have to have this job? Why

couldn't it be like before? You had good ideas and we all were together."

"And we never had money for rent, and we lived in horrible neighbourhoods, and every six months we'd move when I cooked up a scheme that would work best somewhere else. That's no life."

"I liked it."

"You'll see. You'll like this more." Rachel's father gave his daughter a kiss on the forehead. "Don't you think it's about time we went downstairs and started Christmas?"

"I don't know," said Mrs Szeghetti giving Rachel a squeeze. "Feels to me like Christmas has already begun."

With bathrobes and dishevelled hair, the three crept down the stairs together. The plug was pushed in and the tree burst alive, twinkling, glittering, revealing a mound of presents. Rachel sighed happily, then suddenly, noticed something pink and frilly beneath the tree. She scrambled over and gave a shout. "It's a ballerina doll!"

Her father grinned. "I guess Santa knows how much you like ballet!"

Rachel fondled the doll's tight blonde curls and delicate pink tutu. Her face was perfectly formed with rosebud lips and pale skin, tinged with blush. "She's beautiful!"

Her mother handed Rachel a gaily wrapped box. "Sweetie, this one's from me. Merry Christmas!" Opened, the box revealed a blue-green tutu and a leotard edged in sequins. There was a matching head-band, white tights and slippers with a glitter "R" on each toe. Her mother touched the little slipper. "Someday I hope we can afford dancing lessons, but for now—"

"Oh Mommy! I love it! I'll make my own dances!" Rachel laughed. "We've both been making surprises! Wait until you see my presents!" She handed her parents the two special packages.

Carefully undoing the tissue, her mother fingered the tiny stitched flowers, lifted the handkerchief to her cheek. "It's wonderful!" Opening her arms wide, she pulled Rachel to her. "I've never had a more precious gift – a gift from my precious girl."

"Look, Meg. She embroidered my initials." Rachel's father jauntily placed the handkerchief, initials showing, in the pocket of his bathrobe. "So? What do you think? Am I not the handsomest man in Pennyville?" He gave Rachel a big kiss. "I'll take it on trips and think of you."

Her father reached behind the tree. "What's this?" he asked, holding a brown paper package tied with string. Unwrapped, it revealed Clownie, cleaned and sewn, with a new bow around his neck. "How strange!"

"Rachel!" exclaimed her mother. "Were you teasing when you said you lost Clownie? It looks like you fixed him instead."

Rachel touched the new red bow. "I didn't do it."

Her mother said jokingly, "I suppose it was Santa."

"Santa — or magic!" Images raced through her mind as Rachel clutched the little rag doll with the crazy grin and held her belief tight in her heart. There is magic!

Matthew's plaintive cry could be heard from his room.

"I'll go," cried Rachel. "I want to give him Clownie and his bunny and tell him it's Christmas – and how this is going to be a wonderful day!"

She ran upstairs and found Matthew holding the rail to his crib, mournfully bouncing against the bars. "Don't be sad!" she said. "It's Christmas!" Rachel lowered the rail and lifted him free. "Santa left you more presents and I made a surprise for you too." She held him, and for the first time almost liked his morning, sour pee smell. She kissed his honey blonde curls.

Matthew patted her head. "Ay-tel!" he said coyly.

"Is that my name? You said my name!"

Rachel's mother stood in the doorway and smiled.

"Mommy! He said my name!"

"Of course. You're his sister. His good big sister."

Chapter 11

WORDS

The snow, once started, refused to stop. All Christmas day and the next day and the next, the whiteness flew. Rachel built Matthew a snowman with long bunny ears, and Matthew laughed and clapped when she played the clown, falling backwards in the snow. Finally their mittens were soggy cold and it was time for Matthew's nap.

Her parents were listening to an opera record and sitting by the fire. Rachel decided she'd rather go upstairs and draw.

"I never copied those pictures from the newspaper," she told Stripy who was quite disgusted with the cold white stuff covering the ground and had decided to remain inside until it all went away. Old newspapers gave him something interesting to sniff and looked like a nice place to take a snooze. "Off! You goofy cat! These pages are very old and they'll rip!" There again was the picture of the elegant woman and her bird. "Maybe it is Romeo and Miss B!"

After examining the picture carefully, Rachel read the article looking for clues. She sounded out the words, trying to make sense of the rambling sentences. "Beatrice Baumgartner and her internationally renowned and influential father, Captain B, made their appearance at the Ambassadors' Ball hosted by the lovely Lady Astor. The Astors have previously been a guest at the Baumgartner summer mansion in Pennyville."

"It has to be Miss B! Ambassadors! She met ambassadors! And probably kings and queens!" Stripy remained unimpressed.

Sifting through the pile, Rachel found more articles about the "world renowned – breathtakingly beautiful – shining star – the illustrious – Miss Beatrice Baumgartner". She hauled her mother's heavy dictionary upstairs and meticulously looked up every word she didn't understand.

"Knock! Knock!" said her mother coming into the room. "My goodness! You've been quiet for hours!"

Sheepishly, Rachel revealed the old newspapers. "They're from the attic. I've been reading them."

"And using the big dictionary!" exclaimed her mother.

"There're a lot of words I don't understand." Rachel hesitated. "Can I get more papers from the attic? I promise I'll be careful and put them back."

"Yes. Of course. I'm so glad to see you reading!"

Rachel read and read until it was bed-time and her mother insisted she turn out the light.

The next day the sky was vibrant blue. Rachel decided to tromp through the snow and visit Miss B and Sam. Maybe if I ask Miss B about some of the words I don't understand she'll remember things and tell me stories about the past. Then I'll know if she's Beatrice Baumgartner – without her thinking I'm a snoop.

"I approve of your expanding vocabulary," was all Miss B said, after giving curt definitions. "Words give power."

They were drinking tea in the kitchen beside the crackling fire. Miss B took from her cuff the handkerchief with its lopsided stitches. She flushed slightly. "Thank you for the lovely gift."

Sam made motions with his hands. Then, seeing Rachel's puzzlement, he wrote on a small pad, "Thank you!"

Rachel, embarrassed, nodded and smiled.

Miss B resolutely put down her cup. "Would you like to learn more about your words?"

"I suppose," answered Rachel, not sure what the old lady meant.

"We can teach you how to say words in sign language," declared Miss B, excited about the new enterprise. "Truly a beautiful language. I call it 'hand ballet'! First we'll review the basics. We'll do general words and phrases and then next time work on the alphabet. Try and guess the meaning of each gesture," explained Miss B. "Watch the expressions on his face and use your imagination."

Rachel was hoping to uncover the mystery about Miss B's life, but decided it *would* be fun to know a secret way to talk.

Sam made gestures, exaggerating the motions like a game of charades. Rachel would guess and then Sam would write the correct word on a pad of paper. Soon pages were filled with words written in his elaborate handwriting. Sam got sillier and sillier. Rachel laughed so much at his droll and funny ways, she found it difficult to breathe. "I give up! Tell me!"

Miss B pretended to be disgusted with their antics, letting slip only an occasional smile. "You two are impossible!" she declared, and leaning on her cane, left the room. She returned holding a book. "This is for you. A belated Christmas gift. The pages are old and brittle like myself, but you seem a child of fantasy and I thought you might enjoy the reading." She handed Rachel a leather-bound book of fairy tales, containing beautiful illustrations.

"These pictures are great!"

"The words are good as well."

"Thank you," Rachel signed, using her new mode of communication.

As vacation days flew by, Rachel continued her lessons in sign language with Sam and Miss B. She also continued scouring the yellowed papers, searching for clues about her mysterious friends. The newspapers were filled with articles about gold mines out west, and fighting in Europe, and advertisements for ridiculous-looking cars. Rachel became so involved in reading that she often forgot what she was looking for until she stumbled across another article about the wondrous Beatrice Baumgartner.

"I don't understand," Rachel told Stripy. "If Miss B had such an incredible life, why would she hide away for all these years? And who is Sam?" Stripy only closed his eyes to better ponder the questions.

Christmas vacation ended and school resumed. Back at their desks, Rachel smiled at Milly and gave a little wave hello.

Milly responded with enthusiasm – her arm flailing, voice blurting, "Hi! Rachel! Hi!" Everyone stared at Rachel.

I don't care what they think, thought Rachel. Milly's nicer than any of them. And she's a better dancer, too! I'm sick of Lessie bossing me around, telling me everything I do is wrong.

At recess, Rachel approached Milly. "You know – the school has a phonograph and maybe if we promised to be careful, Miss Brigham would let us use it for dancing." Milly nodded, her head bobbing up and down, as she pulled Rachel towards Miss Brigham.

"What a fabulous idea!" exclaimed Miss Brigham. "I'll set it up tomorrow and bring in a few of my old records."

The next day, Lessie was in a fury. "We'll see about that! You're just a bunch of dummies! I know ballet!"

Miss Brigham was patient but firm as she explained. "Lessie. You and your friends have your own activities. I brought the records for Rachel and Milly. You can't be in charge of everything."

Rachel slyly smiled at Lessie, repressing the urge to stick out her tongue. "Come on, Milly. Let's dance!"

Reading group was also a new experience. Rachel found all her hard work deciphering the newspaper had made reading school books seem a cinch.

"You read great!" said Billy Boudreau, impressed as she read using different tones and acting different voices.

When Snapper made fun of Milly's guttural sounds, Rachel whispered fiercely, "Don't you dare!" and he obediently stopped his taunting. Lunchtime, Rachel and Milly now sat together, Rachel helping her read. Milly tried very hard, mouthing the words, but sometimes she just could not comprehend.

"Want to learn a secret language?" Rachel asked.

Milly shook her head and frowned. "Too hard."

"Not this language! It's called 'hand ballet'. You're a dancer. I know you can do it." As Milly slowly learned the motions, the two friends gloried in their ability to talk in class without danger of discovered notes. One day, Billy became curious and asked what they were up to.

"Secrets!" replied Rachel.

"I can see that! Show me how."

After Billy promised not to tease Milly ever again or reveal any of their secrets, Rachel taught him some of the basic signs. He had never been mean like the other kids, and Milly thought he was nice. Snapper made some remark about Billy talking to jerky girls, but Billy punched him on the arm. That seemed to settle it.

School became a happier place. One day Donna asked her a question about homework, and then Susan clapped enthusiastically after Rachel read her poem, and she overheard Snapper saying she was the best artist in class. But most important, Billy Boudreau chose her third for dodge ball and smiled when she scored a point.

The second week in February, Miss Brigham announced the cast for the class play of *Hansel and Gretel*.

"Please let me be Gretel," Rachel wished. But someone else was wishing too. "It's not fair!" Rachel complained to her mother, as they sat playing blocks with Matthew. "Lessie gets everything she wants."

"I'm sure not everything," her mother replied.

"Then how come – just because Lessie's mother told the principal she'd donate the sets and costumes – Lessie's going to be Gretel and I have to be the wicked witch?" Rachel added more blocks to a precarious tower. "Billy's going to be Hansel and Lessie hates Billy. Well, it's not fair, that's all."

Her mother put her arm around Rachel and kissed the top of her head. "You know, your dad did a lot of plays in high school. He was the star, whatever role he had, because he worked hard creating an interesting character. In fact he even had several roles in a small theatre company, before you were born."

"I wish Daddy were here to show me what to do. I hate it when he goes on long sales trips."

"You should go to the library and read about witches. It's the performer, not the part, that makes the star!"

"You mean, if I'm really good, the audience will clap for me more than they clap for Lessie?"

"Well, yes, maybe. But I don't think you understand."

"Yes, I do. I'm going to be the star, not Lessie!"

Chapter 12
SEEDLINGS

Rachel had a plan. She pulled on her mittens, the cool of the key hidden within the fuzz of wool. *If Miss B was a world-famous actress, she can teach me to be a star! I'll tell her I found the newspapers. She can't get that mad.* The sidewalk was icy and narrow between the waist-high frozen drifts. Within the garden, trees bent low, and the cherub on the bird-bath was hidden beneath the thick, white weight.

Sam bowed his usual greeting and then asked, in sign, "How are you?"

"OK. Well, not really. I have to ask Miss B something and I'm a little nervous."

Sam nodded and signed, "I understand."

Near the kitchen, they entered a small bright sun room, hung with ferns. Miss B, in a dress of burgundy velvet, was seated on a white wicker chair and surrounded by floral pillows. Figaro lay curled on her lap.

Rachel sat on the matching wicker couch, awkwardly contemplating what she would say. Tea was brought and they exchanged their usual pattern of pleasantries.

Finally, Rachel blurted, "I'm going to be the witch in our play, *Hansel and Gretel*!"

"How nice," replied Miss B, taking a sip of tea.

"Well," continued Rachel, "I wondered, if you could show me how to be a good witch."

Miss B's eyes twinkled. "I always thought the witch in *Hansel and Gretel* was rather bad."

"That's not exactly what I meant." Rachel took a sip of tea and shifted uncomfortably in her chair. "See – I think – maybe – you used to be a famous actress – and I want you to teach me how to act!"

Miss B put down her tea with a clatter. "To whom have you been talking?" Her voice was hard and sharp.

Rachel paused, then chose the truth. "No one. I read it in some old newspapers I found."

Miss B scowled. "I had forgotten. What else do these old newspapers say?"

"Oh, wonderful things!" gushed Rachel. "All about your travels and performances and elegant balls. The drawings of you are really beautiful!"

"You read nothing else?" she asked, suspiciously.

Rachel shook her head. "Nothing in particular. See, I want you to show me how to be so great on stage that I'm the star and everyone claps loudest for me!"

Miss B relaxed, slightly, back into her chair. "Wild

applause is a most satisfying sound. It penetrates your very bone, no words of praise can ever match the feeling." Her voice grew faint. "Sometimes I hear its echo in my vacant rooms or at the top of stairs." She turned to Rachel with her intent glare. "Now you hunger for the same acclaim. Have you talent?"

Hesitantly, Rachel replied, "I think so."

"Nonsense!" bellowed Miss B, thumping the floor with her cane. The black and white cat leapt off the chair. "If you have talent, *say* so, proclaim yourself, stop slouching and pulling on your braid. I repeat — do you have talent?"

Rachel sat up straight and looked Miss B in the eye. "I know I can act like a witch."

"I believe you. We'll find the witch within and direct its path of expression."

"Does that mean you'll help me?"

"Yes, you shall be my apprentice."

"Oh! Miss B! I'm the luckiest girl in the whole wide world!"

"There exists no light without shadow. Hansel and Gretel need the witch. Stardom has its pain. Bring your script tomorrow and we will rehearse. Today, I am tired."

Sam smiled and motioned with his hands.

"House with green?" Rachel questioned, puzzled.

"He wants to show you his favourite place — other than the kitchen. Go on! Follow him," snapped Miss B, brushing the cat hairs off her dress. "Perhaps now I can have a moment's peace."

Sam enfolded Rachel's hand in his huge paw and led her through chilly halls to a door in the back of the house. They opened the door and entered another land. Hot and humid, filled with light, the long glass room arched high above them. Tables overflowing with plants lined either side and down the middle. Outside, Rachel could see the snow piled high.

"Oh, Sam! It's beautiful!"

"Yes. Beautiful," Sam motioned with his hands.

"Beautiful," Rachel repeated with her hands.

Patiently, Sam her showed her how to thin the rows of seedlings, pinch dead leaves and repot root-bound plants.

As Rachel watered and gently pruned the plants with Sam, the thought kept racing through her mind, I'm going to be Miss B's apprentice. I'm going to be a star!

"I understand why this is your favourite place," said Rachel. "Can I come and help you again?"

"Of course," Sam signed.

They heard the approaching thumping of Miss B's cane. She entered, Figaro swishing around her legs. "Goodness! You two! Do you have any idea of the time?"

"You're right! I've got to run!" said Rachel. "See you tomorrow – with my script!"

The next day after school, Rachel threw her books on the couch and ran off to rehearse with Miss B.

"Where are you going?" asked her mother.

"The library," Rachel promptly lied, feeling suddenly ashamed to see her mother's happy look. To make the lie convincing, Rachel ran through the park to the library, took out a book on witches and headed for her visit to Miss B and Sam.

I wish they didn't have to be a secret. I don't like to lie. She thought of the dark mansion, of Sam's contorted face and the sometimes fearsome manner of Miss B. Maybe she is right, not to want anyone to know. Mom's even scared of regular people – she'd never let me be friends with someone like Miss B or Sam. She only wants me to be friends with "nice" little girls my own age. Maybe if I'm a big success in the play, I can tell her how Miss B helped me and Mom will think it's OK.

Rehearsal was difficult.

"Stand up straight!" demanded Miss B. "Look me in the eye! How do you ever hope to project the image of a witch if you insist on slouching and chewing on your braid!"

Near tears, Rachel tried her best, going over and over her lines, struggling with Miss B's sharp commands.

"Stop feeling sorry for yourself," Miss B retorted, when Rachel complained. "Nothing of value is ever accomplished without effort. Easy goals, any idiot can obtain! You are rushing! This is not a contest of speed! Breathe! Enunciate your words!"

Sam came in and suggested a break for tea. Miserably, Rachel took her cup. On the saucer was a note, written in Sam's curlicued and florid style – "Good work!"

She looked up at him and smiled.

After tea, Miss B showed Rachel some exercises to

increase her energy and they practised voice by making different sounds. Exhausted, Rachel promised to return the next day and continue her lessons.

Rachel was late for dinner, but her mother quickly forgave when she saw the library book. "I understand how you can lose track of time. When I was your age, the library was my favourite place. You don't know how pleased I am to see you enjoy reading! And look! I have a surprise for you!"

"Daddy!" Rachel threw her arms around his neck.

"My goodness, you're getting tall! Have you been doing spells to make you grow? Mom says you're practising to be a witch!"

"And I'm going to be great! Maybe. I have to work on my cackle and remember not to chew my braids."

Mr Szeghetti laughed. "Yessirree! Not chewing braids is a lesson all actors must learn. Did I ever tell you about the time I played Robin Hood? My fancy sword work was what won your mother's heart. The competition was run off by my mighty blade! Isn't that true?" he asked, kissing his wife on the neck.

"Oh, Alfred!" Mrs Szeghetti giggled. "Time for dinner!"

Rachel patted her mashed potatoes into a smooth perfect circle, trying to imagine her parents before she was born. I wonder what Mom did before she started the bookkeeping for extra money? Rachel knew that the "extra money" was all they lived on sometimes. Those piles of big black books had been spread across the kitchen table for as long as she could remember. Carefully she rolled her peas so they formed a border around her potatoes. I wonder if Mom ever wanted to do something exciting?

"Rachel!" exclaimed her mother. "Don't play with your food."

"You need lots of nourishment," agreed her father. "Performing your best uses up lots of calories." He sighed wistfully, and patted his rounded belly. "Much more than sales."

Mrs Szeghetti reached for her husband's hand. "You work very hard and still look handsome to me."

I'm going to work real hard and never give up, Rachel vowed. I'm going to be great. I am.

Chapter 13

WISHES

The next time Rachel went to Miss B's, she was prepared for the rigorous tutoring. She spoke strongly, cackled with authentic glee and never once chewed on her braid.

"Hmnpf," was Miss B's comment as they sat down to tea and fresh-baked cookies. "You might have the makings of a performer after all. We'll see."

The seedlings in the greenhouse grew tall enough to be transferred to individual pots and buds began to appear on the largest orchid. The days became warmer and Rachel became more and more confident of her role as a witch. Lately, every time Rachel felt shy and insecure, Miss B's voice would echo in her mind – "Stop slouching! Look people in the eye!" Now, Rachel almost never chewed her braid and her voice was stronger as she spoke in class. The courage stone does work, she thought. I like the me I'm making.

All through February and March, the class rehearsed after lunch in the auditorium. Milly was a dancing gingerbread girl.

"Your spins were really good this time," Rachel whispered to her as they walked in line back to class. "Much better than anything Lessie can do. My mom asked me if I wanted to invite all the girls to my birthday party, but they're not my friends." The line marched by the office. "Although Susan's been OK lately."

"Yes," Milly signed. "Nice."

"But she probably wouldn't come unless Lessie did. Would you want to come to my party? With just my family?"

"Yes! Yes!" Milly exclaimed loudly. "A party! I want to come!"

The crabby office lady popped out her door. "No talking in the halls! Who wants detention?"

"Trouble," Milly signed.

"Witch," signed Rachel.

That night, Rachel sat in her room, copying the picture of the parrot from the newspaper as a present for Miss B. What will my parents think of Milly? She does act a little different.

The ballerina doll, new and untouched, stood poised on Rachel's dresser. The doll's face seemed cold and haughty – not beautiful at all. I wouldn't want to be like her, thought Rachel. Even if she is a ballerina. Milly is my friend, but so are Miss B and Sam. She imagined them all coming to her party, knocking on her door, viewing the drab, boring house and ragged furniture. No. I'd like them to meet my parents – but not here.

I know! Miss B and Sam can come see me in the show! Then I'll explain to my parents how Miss B taught me how to be a star and Mom and Dad will be so happy, they'll let us be friends and I won't have to lie any more! It would be good for Miss B and Sam to get out for a change. People will see she's not a scary witch and Sam's not a monster, but very sweet. I bet that's why everyone thinks she's strange – they've just never seen her! And now they will! Happily, Rachel returned to her drawing, imagining the big event.

On Rachel's birthday, winter bequeathed a final veil of snow. She received other gifts as well – hugs, kisses, blueberry pancakes and presents from her family. Her mother gave her a beautiful teal-coloured party dress and a book about a pig and spider. Inside was inscribed, "To my wonderful daughter, artist – and reader."

"And I brought you a dancing partner," her father said.

It was a funny ballerina marionette, with a wide grin and braids sticking straight out from either side of her head.

"I found her in an antique shop," he explained, twirling his moustache. "She reminded me of you."

Matthew, with help from Mom, bought her a pair of purple mittens. After breakfast, she amused Matthew by dancing the ballerina over the living room furniture. Matthew giggled and squealed and danced Clownie.

"Are you trying to be like me?" said Rachel. "Copying your big sister?" She danced the marionette over to Clownie and had the ballerina give the clown a kiss.

Rachel's mother came in, wiping her hands on her apron. Her eyes shone. "I'm busy with something in the kitchen. Maybe you should try your new mittens and go outside."

"Can I take Mattie?"

"I suppose. We'll dress him warmly and put him in the wagon – not enough snow for his sled."

Matthew's and Rachel's cheeks were soon rosy in the winter–spring air. Rachel sang silly songs and slid in the melting snow to make Matthew laugh. She wiped his nose when it got drippy and made a snow-ball for him to hold.

"It'll be nice when you can talk and we can do more things – make fun of Daddy's silly jokes, hide your peas in your napkin – like friends. Maybe some-day you'll meet Miss B and Sam. They're very special. Don't tell anybody, but I'm going to ask them to my show."

"Rachel!" called her mother. "It's almost time for your friend, Milly, to arrive!"

"Coming!" answered Rachel.

Matthew almost fell off the wagon as she sped inside. Their cold noses were greeted with smells of baking cake and sizzling French fries. The dining room was filled with balloons and streamers. Rachel slipped on her new dress and skipped downstairs. She was in the kitchen, trying to decide whether to sneak a peek at the cake, when the doorbell rang. Rachel ran to open the door for Milly.

Milly, present clasped to her chest, stood smiling as her mother prodded her. "Millicent, say Happy Birthday!"

"Happy Birthday!" repeated Milly.

Rachel's mother came downstairs with Matthew. Rachel took Milly's hand. "Mom, remember? This is Milly."

"I'm glad to see you again."

"Thank you so much for inviting Millicent," Milly's mother began. "It means so much – it isn't often—"

Rachel wished Milly's mother would stop talking and go away. She signed to Milly, "Boring!" Milly giggled.

"Well, I'll leave you two alone," concluded Milly's mother, turning to go. "Have fun. Millicent, don't forget your gift."

Milly smiled shyly and handed Rachel the present. "Happy Birthday," she whispered.

Rachel unwrapped a record of *Swan Lake*. "This is great! It's the same as the one we play in school!"

Milly beamed happily. "What a lovely present!" agreed Rachel's mother. "Well, I'd better get back to the kitchen, if we're ever going to eat."

"Howdy!" said Rachel's father, bringing in a load

of wood. "Last fire of the season. You two girls any good at rubbing sticks together?"

Rachel groaned. "Daddy, you use matches!"

"Matches? Oh, yes, matches. I forgot. You must be Milly. Excuse my paw, it's a trifle dirty." Milly giggled and put both her hands behind her back.

"Come on," said Rachel, "let's go up to my room."

Upstairs, the two friends explored Rachel's treasures. Milly especially liked the ballerina outfit Rachel's mother made for Christmas and insisted on trying it on.

"You look beautiful!" Rachel said, as Milly admired herself in the mirror. Rachel took a hanger, and like a magic wand, touched Milly lightly on the shoulder.

"Milly – the beautiful ballerina! Greatest dancer in the world!" Very seriously, Milly stared at the image in the mirror, and nodded.

"Party time!" called Rachel's mother.

Milly wore the costume downstairs. Rachel's father whistled and her mother said, "Very pretty! I've heard you're a good dancer!"

Milly solemnly curtsied in reply.

They ate Rachel's favourite foods – French fries, pigs-in-a-blanket, red Jello with baby oranges, and two cans of black olives.

"Presenting – the Dancing Olive Sisters!" Rachel and Milly put olives on all ten fingers, waltzed them over the table – then ate them one by one. The cake was banana cream with banana frosting, decorated with tiny ballerinas and pink roses.

"Make a wish before those ballerinas turn old and grey!" her father coaxed.

Rachel closed her eyes and silently wished. Please! Please! Please! Let Miss B and Sam come to my play!

The candles were blown out in one big breath.

Chapter 14
SCARS

It was several days later when Rachel slipped through the hidden door to the mansion. Courage stone in her pocket, she was confident in her mission. *Miss B said I was her best student – they've got to come to my play!*

"Hello, Romeo!" Rachel called gaily to the parrot as Sam led her into the kitchen.

Miss B sat at the table cracking walnuts with a gold nutcracker. "Sit down, my dear. Sam and I could use the help of youthful hands. Each year the shells seem tougher." Miss B chuckled. "Much like myself, I'm afraid."

"Miss B, I wanted to ask if you'd do something – something that would really mean a lot to me."

"My dear, you need lessons in decorum. Before

you ask a favour, it is proper to say, 'How do you do?' and then engage in a certain amount of idle chat. Here is a pile of nuts and the utensils with which they may be cracked."

Rachel took a nut and nutcracker and squeezed until there was a satisfying crunch. "I'm sorry I didn't say hello – but it's important."

"Patience is a virtue ignored by youth. Well, out with it! I can see you will persist."

Rachel began her often rehearsed speech. "I really appreciate how you've helped me learn how to act, and I think you're a great teacher – and – and I really want you and Sam to come see me in the show."

Miss B pursed her lips and cracked a nut.

"It won't be the same if you aren't there," continued Rachel. "No one else understands. Will you come? Please?" Nervously, Rachel began to eat some of the pieces.

"Those are for cooking and not to be eaten," ordered Miss B. "Your manners are atrocious."

"I'm sorry. But can you come? Will you?"

"Of course not! Such an impudent question! What makes you think you can march in here and demand we come wherever you please. I am not at your beck and call."

"It might be fun to get out and see my school—"

"*Fun!*" interrupted Miss B. "*Never!* My life is fulfilled within these walls – away from prying eyes. Those who professed to love me saw only roles I played. Those who hated me tied my name to untruthful shame. Here, I need only the mirror of a true friend." Miss B turned to Sam, and for a moment

113

her stern face was gentle. "You have been allowed admittance to our sanctuary. The privilege is not to be abused with unreasonable requests. I will never, under any circumstances, leave these grounds. I will not submit myself to stupid, gossipy mouths and mean, malicious minds." Miss B handed Rachel a nut. "You have been an adept student. I'm sure your performance will be spectacular."

"How will *you* ever know?" Rachel blurted out.

The kettle began to whistle.

"My dear, I can understand your disappointment. These emotions, however, will destroy your performance."

"You don't understand!" yelled Rachel, shooting up from her chair and banging the table with her fist. "You say you're my friend, but friends don't make friends lie! Remember what you said about truth? And the courage stone? You told me – stand up tall, don't care what people say."

Rachel felt the full force of her anger – and her strength. "What's hard about coming to my school play? You act so wise and better than anyone else, but you're just like Lessie! Everything has to be your way. You always have to be the boss!" Rachel fell back into her chair.

Miss B massaged her knotted hands. "Are you quite finished with your outburst?"

"I'm sorry," murmured Rachel. "I didn't mean to get so angry. I take it back."

"Unfortunately, words cannot be reeled in like some flapping fish on a line. You will leave – and never enter this house again!"

"But – Miss B!"

"I said *leave!*" Grasping tightly to the arm of the chair, she pushed herself to standing. Composure regained, she swept cat hairs from her skirt, and left the room.

Trembling, Rachel walked to the front door.

Sam walked with her. In the hall, he handed Rachel her hat and mittens. They stood awkwardly a moment. Then Sam reached and tenderly touched the tear on Rachel's cheek with his large weathered hand. His other hand lay on his chest.

Rachel looked into his scarred, distorted face and saw the glistening eye and curled lip of half a smile. She touched his hand upon her cheek. "I know you're my friend."

The air brought the smell of spring pushing through the dark of winter, but Rachel's heart felt filled with ice.

The next day, she angrily collected all the old newspapers and returned them to the attic. "I hate her! She's mean and stupid! What do I need her for, anyway? I was dumb to ever believe in her!" Dust billowed as she threw the newspapers into the trunk.

She was lowering herself down the ladder, when she spied a trunk deep within the shadow of the eaves. She'd never noticed this one before. Probably some more dumb newspapers telling lies about the "wonderful Miss Beatrice Baumgartner". But, thought Rachel, it wouldn't hurt to look. Unlike the others, this trunk was locked. Rachel pulled and banged until the rotten wood gave way. "More newspapers!" she said with disgust. Then she read the headline. In huge bold letters they proclaimed: HUNDREDS DIE IN THEATRE FIRE. LOCAL HEIRESS CHARGED.

The light grew dim as Rachel read the papers from the locked trunk. Black marks streaked her cheeks as she wiped her tears with dusty hands. Why didn't she tell me? I didn't understand! How could the town say the fire was Miss B's fault? What does "gross negligence" mean? How could she help it if the lamps she ordered from Italy burst into flames. The fire chief said, "She was repeatedly warned of the dangers but insisted that the recommended safe lamps were not elegant enough for her theatre." That's not her fault! And I'm sure she was just being nice letting everyone in who wanted to see the show – even if there weren't any more seats. Miss B was a big star and they were her fans. She didn't need the money – she was rich.

Rachel thought of other facts she had gleaned from her hoard of newspapers. How Miss B's mother had died when Miss B was a little girl. How Miss B's father, Captain Baumgartner, had built this estate as a vacation home. How he had died a few years before the fire and Miss B was the only heir. Rachel remembered the first day she met Miss B and how they had planted the tulip together. Miss B had lost her mother – not just a mouse!

All the puzzle pieces were coming together. Rachel hunted through the other papers. She found one dated two months later that told of the "immensely wealthy ageing actress who was forced by the courts to relinquish the majority of her country estate to make a city park." Dante's Park used to be her own

116

gigantic back yard. Rachel gazed around the attic. That's why this house is called the Caretaker's. This must be her house as well. The fire was June 13, 1919. She built the wall almost forty years ago. How could someone live all by herself for so long? The next sentence explained part of the reason.

The once popular actress was booed off the stage and has vowed never again to return to the theatre. She will be staying in Pennyville and selling the rest of her apartments and estates. Nurses from the hospital have been reporting on her daily visits to the young gardener who was so tragically burned while saving her life. Speculations as to the nature of their relationship have been widely discussed.

That must have been Sam! Rachel shuddered with the thought of flames searing his face into that frightful mask. Miss B gave up acting and stayed with Sam!

Rachel put the papers back in the trunk and came down from the attic. There must be a way I can get back to Miss B. Sam's not mad at me. If I go and talk to him, maybe he can explain to Miss B that I know all the secrets and understand why she didn't want to come. Maybe he can tell her how sorry I am that I yelled. Maybe he can tell her how I want to still be friends.

Pale yellow crocuses pushed up around grimy patches of melting snow as she entered the awakening garden. The earth along the path was soft and muddy. She tapped gently on the greenhouse glass. Sam, busy tending plants, hurried to let her in. He glanced nervously over his shoulder, then smiled and pointed to an orchid beginning to bloom.

"It's gorgeous!" Rachel exclaimed.

Sam put his fingers to his lips.

"I understand," Rachel whispered, sadly. "I know the secret."

Sam signed, "Which secret?"

"I found the old newspapers. I know about the fire and how you got burned. How you jumped up on to the stage and wrapped your coat over Miss B and led her through the flames. I know about the trial and what people said." Sam nodded and plucked dead leaves from an orchid.

"I didn't know all that when I asked her to come to the show. Can't you talk to her? Explain how sorry I am? Explain how we're friends and shouldn't stay mad."

Sam spoke rapidly with his hands.

"Too many words I don't know! You're going too fast!" Rachel protested.

Sam took out his notepad and wrote with florid penmanship: Forgive. There is pain you can never understand. Time changes many things, but some scars are for ever.

Rachel could hear the thump of Miss B's cane as she approached from down the hall. It was almost time for tea. Sam motioned, "You must go!"

"But—" Rachel began.

Sam opened the door that led outside. "You must go!"

"Please, Sam," Rachel pleaded as she stepped from

the humid greenhouse into the cool dusk air. "Aren't we friends?"

But Sam had already closed the door.

I wish I were a real witch, thought Rachel, so I could cast a spell. "But it's no use!" she sobbed out loud, as she ran through the garden. "There is no magic! Miracles aren't real! People are stupid and mean and bad things happen and nothing can ever make it better! I thought they were my friends — but they aren't! I don't have any friends and probably never will," she proclaimed to the crow sitting on the wall above the door. "And I don't care. So there!"

She turned to look back towards the mansion hidden behind the budding trees and awakening earth. "I do care," she said quietly. "I'll miss you and I'll never forget all the good things you said."

Chapter 15
STAR

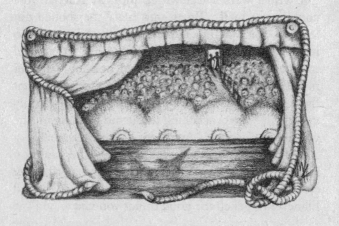

Rachel stood in the empty lot, outside the door she had locked for the very last time. Along the wall pussy willows grew, their buds all silvery velvet. Rachel stroked the little grey furs. "You are so pretty – like tiny sleeping mice." My mouse-tulip! she remembered with an ache. I'll never see it bloom! She imagined the pointy green shoot pushing through its winter nest of leaves – reaching for new life. Breathing in the mudpie air, Rachel smiled, picturing how excitedly her mother was greeting each new sign of spring. Mom is happier here. She likes having a house with a fireplace and trees. Dad says this summer he'll be home more and next year he'll have a better route. I'm glad we're staying. Maybe we can start a little garden, and next fall plant tulip bulbs! Rachel broke off an armful of pussy willows and ran home.

The kitchen smelled of roast chicken. Rachel's mother was at the sink snapping the ends off asparagus. Rachel presented the bouquet and wrapped her arms around her mother's waist.

"My, my!" exclaimed her mother. "What's all this?"

"Pussy willows," replied Rachel, grinning proudly.

"Why they are the most beautiful pussy willows I have ever seen!"

"I knew you'd like them." Rachel sat down at the table. "Mom, can we have tea? Use the good teapot and china cups?"

Her mother laughed and wiped her hands on her apron. "I didn't know you liked tea! My best friend, when I was little, was Dutch. Her mother would call us in with her funny accent, 'Nettie! Meggie! Come to tea!' " Rachel's mother smiled as she set the kettle on to boil and rinsed the blue tea pot. "You can use my old cup with the painted forget-me-nots."

"What happened to her?" asked Rachel. "Your friend."

"She moved. I moved. It's hard to stay in touch."

"Do you miss her?"

"Yes – I do. She was a good friend."

"Mommy, I know you like it here – but are you ever lonely?"

The kettle whistled and Rachel's mother poured the water into the pot. "I'm usually too busy to be lonely," she said, bringing two flowered cups and sitting down at the table.

"But sometimes, don't you want a friend?"

"I have friends who write letters, though lately only at Christmas. You know – I'm kind of shy." She sighed and clasped Rachel's hand. "Oh, Rachel! I had hoped it would be easier for you. I'm sorry we have moved so much and it's hard for you to make friends."

"Mommy," said Rachel. "I've got to tell you something. What I said wasn't always true. I did have friends for a little while, not just Milly. Next door – I made friends with Miss B and Sam, but she was afraid of people talking about her, so I promised not to tell. But now we're not friends any more. I'm sorry, Mommy. I felt bad to lie."

Rachel's mother touched her cup. "That was where you learned to like tea and how to embroider, wasn't it?"

Rachel nodded.

"I knew about your friendship. One day, putting clothes in your room, I looked out the window. You were with her in the garden. I was very upset and told your father. He convinced me to let it be. Said you needed to try your wings and do things without us interfering. You were so sad back then and always seemed happier when you returned." Her mother took a sip of tea. "Your dad did some investigating and decided they were two lonely people who were probably enjoying your visits as well. He told me about the trouble they'd had and figured that's why you weren't saying anything. I've noticed how much you've changed. They must be good friends."

Rachel pulled on her braid. "Were. Miss B got mad 'cause I asked her to the show. Actually – she got mad because I yelled and told her she was like Lessie!

Miss B seems so smart – why does she sometimes act so stupid?"

"Nobody's perfect. Even heroes are flawed. Appreciate the good and forgive the bad. It's all we can do."

Rachel smiled. "You sound like Miss B."

Her mother laughed. "Can I be your hero too? It made me sad to know someone else was being better at making you happy. But at the time, I was feeling rather overwhelmed. I'm sorry."

"Oh Mommy!" Rachel went around the table, sat on her lap and hugged her close. "I love you!"

"I love you too."

"At least you'll come to my play and see me be a star!"

"You already are a star. My star."

The night of the performance, Rachel and her family hurried up the steps to school.

"I'm going to save seats," said her father, taking Matthew. "I'll meet you inside."

"It feels strange to be here at night," Rachel told her mother. "It smells different, like wax and polish instead of kids and cafeteria."

The dressing room was a hubbub of costumes and excited voices. Rachel's mother gave a kiss on the black wig Rachel was squeezing over her hair. "You'll be great."

Soon the class gathered behind the closed curtain. The rumble of the crowd bounced around in Rachel's stomach.

"This is performance night," said Miss Brigham in

a loud whisper, "which means no fooling around. Donna and Milly, my gingerbread children, when you dance at the end, cover more of the stage. Snapper! Stop immediately, or you will be a woodcutter without an axe!"

Rachel touched her long putty nose and adjusted the elastic on her pointed hat. She wiggled her fingers and toes for energy as Miss B had taught her to do. Lessie just swishes around in her dress, thought Rachel, smugly. She's not really acting at all.

"One minute until curtain," said Miss Brigham. "If you forget your lines, I'll say them softly from the wings. Places everyone, and break a leg!"

Milly was clutching the backdrop with bewildered, scared eyes.

Rachel signed to her, "Don't worry. You're a beautiful ballerina – the best dancer in the world!"

Milly nodded. Rachel crouched in her candy witch's house hidden behind a painted set of trees. Please let *me* do OK, she wished.

The audience became quiet. The curtain rose. Billy had the first line. He spoke loud and clear. Then there was silence.

Lessie must have forgotten her lines, thought Rachel.

Miss Brigham's voice came from backstage, then Lessie spoke, repeating the words in a shaky squeak. Billy said his next line. Again there was silence, then Miss Brigham's voice, then the low shaky squeak. I knew she'd freeze, thought Rachel. Her curls may be in place, but she can't act.

Every one of Lessie's line's throughout the scene,

Miss Brigham had to whisper. Birds came and ate the bread crumbs and angels protected the children while they slept. The painted set of trees was pulled away, revealing the candy house.

"Look, Gretel," said Billy. "How delicious it looks!"

Lessie was supposed to argue with Billy, then decide to eat a candy cane. That was Rachel's cue. She heard a noise and saw Snapper, backstage, fooling with his axe. Suddenly he tripped, slammed his head against a metal pulley. Blood gushed from his forehead. Miss Brigham motioned for the children to continue as she hurried Snapper away.

Billy and Lessie were alone down stage. There was no voice of Miss Brigham coming from the wings. The audience began to murmur as the silence continued. Rachel remembered what Miss B had taught her: "The show must go on! Never break character!"

"Nibble nibble, mousekins, who's nibbling on my housekins?" she cackled, peering around the door.

Lessie stood, pale as a ghost, gripping Billy's hand. Any satisfaction Rachel felt in Lessie's humbled state, disappeared when she saw her pained expression.

"I can see, little girl, you think my house is delicious, but you'd like some dinner as well," Rachel said, improvizing. "I will feed you a sumptuous feast."

Billy caught on fast and they took turns leading Lessie around the stage and saying her lines. Rachel discreetly pointed to Lessie and signed "cage". Billy nodded and Gretel went into the cage instead of Hansel. Sometimes Rachel floundered inventing lines, but she stayed in character, cackling and gesturing dramatically.

I'm doing it! I'm being great! thought Rachel. If only Miss B and Sam were here! Hansel pushed Rachel the witch into the oven and she let out a blood curdling scream. She hid within the oven, her excitement ready to explode the cardboard walls.

The lilting voices of the gingerbread children began their song. I hope Milly is doing OK, Rachel worried. The sound of their voices waved about as they danced around the stage. Then the song was over but the moving continued. The audience began to clap, increasing until it became a rhythmic beat. This wasn't in the script, thought Rachel. The clapping erupted into thunderous applause. Snapper, bandaged, reunited with his children and the curtain went down. Quickly, Rachel climbed out of the oven and ran to centre stage to take Billy and Lessie's hands.

"What happened?" she whispered to Billy.

"Milly danced."

The cast bowed together, then each character stepped forward. The audience clapped and clapped, but when Milly stepped in front, the audience went wild. Whistles and cheers filled the auditorium. Milly is the star, not me, Rachel admitted, as jealousy bit into the glow of success.

After the final bow, everyone whooped and jumped around. A lot of kids clustered around Milly, congratulating her. Milly, stunned, grinned and nodded.

126

Rachel watched and inwardly moaned. It's not fair. She didn't even have any lines, She wasn't supposed to keep dancing. I should have been the star, not Milly.

Chapter 16
FRIENDS

Parents and friends poured from the auditorium on to the crowded stage. Rachel noticed Lessie silently slip away as she saw her parents approach. They stood with stretched smiles, accepting people's awkward compliments – for the costumes and set.

"Rachel!" called her mother, rushing over. "My wonderful witch! I was so proud!"

Rachel's father gave her a kiss on the ear. "I guess my place as the family 'ham' has been usurped."

Matthew reached over and pulled at Rachel's hat. When Rachel turned to kiss him, he whimpered.

"It's just me," she said, tickling his tummy.

Miss Brigham was flying around, congratulating everyone. "Rachel! You were absolutely perfect for your part! Wasn't she wonderful? She and Billy really thought on their feet and saved the show."

Rachel felt a bit of the glow return.

"I appreciate what a friend you've been to Milly this year," added Miss Brigham. "I know you must be very proud." Miss Brigham gave Rachel a loving squeeze on the shoulder, then whisked off to speak to other parents.

The touch on Rachel's shoulder filled her with warmth. Milly does have a harder time, thought Rachel. All she can do is dance. I'm good at lots of things.

"It's late, my little witchy," said Rachel's mother. "And your little witch brother needs his nappy changed. Go get your things and we'll meet you by the front entrance."

As Rachel pushed through the throng, she felt a familiar grasp. Milly's eyes were smiling and wide.

"Good witch, Rachel."

"And you're a great dancer," Rachel replied. "The greatest in the whole wide world!"

Milly nodded and then signed, "Friend!"

"Yes," Rachel signed back. "Friend!"

Susan walked by with her older sister. "You were a fantastic witch," said Susan.

"Yeah," agreed her sister. "You almost scared me!"

Rachel thanked them and bounced down the halls.

Billy gave her the thumbs-up sign. "That was great what you did. I didn't know what to do!"

Rachel blushed. "Yes you did. You were great too."

"Well, anyway – see ya around."

"Yeah. See ya."

Her glow was bright as she entered the dressing

room. Lessie was the only one there, costume off, neatly folded on a chair. She looked strange in school dress, still wearing heavy make-up. Rachel began to gather her clothes.

"You were good," said Lessie, glaring. "I wasn't."

Rachel shifted uncomfortably, wishing someone else would enter the room.

Lessie continued. "I guess I'm supposed to say thanks. You saved the show."

"It's – it's OK," Rachel stammered.

Lessie gave Rachel a disdainful look, picked up her clothes and went towards the door. She stopped.

"Those are for you." She gestured with her head towards the dressing table. "I thought they were for me so I opened the card. They were for you." The door slammed behind her.

On the table, was a card, a spectacular orchid and a brown paper package tied with string. In the package were walnut cookies. The card read – "For Rachel, from your friends" and was written in a familiar hand.

"Rachel! Rachel! You've got to come quick!" cried Susan. "They said they wanted you!"

The two girls raced back to the stage. There was a strange, low buzzing – the sound of many whispers.

Slowly, more regally and steady than Rachel had ever seen her, Miss B walked down the aisle, Sam at her side. The scattered audience watched as the strange pair mounted the steps. Rachel felt the world spin.

Miss B stood before her, both hands on her cane.

"Congratulations, my dear. You were wonderful."

Rachel grasped the knotted fingers. "I wished so

hard that you would come!" She clasped Sam's giant hand and holding on to her two friends, she called, "Miss Brigham! I'd like you to meet my other teachers, Miss Beatrice Baumgartner and Sam."

Rachel could feel Miss B's hand grip with fear.

Miss Brigham smiled and came with arm extended. "How lovely for you to make the effort to see our little show." She shook Miss B's hand. "I hope this will not be the only time we are honoured with your presence."

Then, for the first time ever, Rachel saw Miss B stumble for a reply.

"I really never—" Miss B began. "Rachel is quite – I am pleased to have been her teacher."

As Miss B spoke, Rachel suddenly saw her as a frail, very human, very old woman. Beyond the fiery eyes and powerful manner was someone who had been weakened by life. But Rachel knew in that moment that she was someone who, unquestionably, was her own "inevitable product".

"Oh! Miss B! I love you!" Rachel threw her arms around Miss B's neck and kissed the withered cheek.

Miss B's lips quivered and she fumbled in her purse.

"Rachel!" called her mother, coming from behind the wings. "What's taking you so long?" She stopped amazed.

Rachel was hugging Sam and Miss B was wiping her eyes with her hand-stitched embroidered handkerchief.

"We wondered – where you were," her mother stammered.

131

Rachel's father followed, holding Matthew. "Well, well! I guess we missed the second act!"

"Mommy, Daddy, these are our neighbours, my friends – Miss B and Sam." Grinning, Rachel added, "Miss B and Sam – I'd like you to meet my family!"

Some people approached Miss B. They all began, "I am the son of—" or "I am the granddaughter of—" or "I am the great-grand niece of so-and-so." Cordially, Miss B smiled and said, "How do you do," while Sam stood tight beside her.

Rachel watched, happily, as her no longer secret friends became re-introduced to the world of Pennyville.

Eventually Miss B began to tire and bid everyone goodnight. Rachel's family walked with them to their ancient, elegant car.

"I am so happy you came," said Rachel.

"So am I, my dear. So am I. Sam convinced me. We spoke of many things." A breeze fluttered new leaves as Miss B explained. "I plånned to sit, hidden in back of the theatre, then quietly depart. But when I saw you rise to the occasion, I was so proud – I had to tell you immediately – in that moment after a performance when all stands still." Miss B awkwardly touched her cameo brooch. "I have been a silly old woman. Sometimes, what I would like to think of as strength is really childish stubbornness." Her voice caught slightly. "Are we still friends?"

"Oh, Miss B! Of course we are! I missed you so!"

Miss B nodded and smiled. "Well, then. As a form of an apology, I'd like to invite you all to tea – perhaps Sunday, at three, in the garden?"

On the morning of Miss B's tea party, Rachel scrubbed extra clean and wore ribbons in her braids to match her dress. Matthew was outfitted like a little sailor and Mr Szeghetti wore his suit. Mrs Szeghetti fussed with her hair, couldn't decide on a hat and insisted Rachel wear white cotton gloves.

Sam, looking uncomfortable and nervous in a yellowed white linen suit, was waiting at the front gate to let them in. He gave his usual bow and led them along the path.

Rachel slipped her hand in his. "Sam. It's only me. Funny not to climb the wall or come by the back door."

Miss B was dressed in white lace with a small nosegay of violets pinned at the edge of her collar. The elegantly draped table was set in the garden near the fountain where Rachel had first met her.

"Please, be seated," said Miss B, as Sam pulled back the chairs.

"You certainly have one hell of a spectacular garden!" exclaimed Mr Szeghetti, bending over to smell a hyacinth.

Mrs Szeghetti looked aghast and hastily added, "I've never been in a place more beautiful!"

Miss B poured the tea. Figaro purred and rubbed against the table leg. Daffodils posed in a crystal vase, while sailboat-shaped napkins set ready to sail serenely off the cloth. There were little sandwiches with the crust cut off, and berry tarts and fancy cakes – and a long, awkward silence.

Rachel's father clutched his delicate cup as if at any moment it would crumble in his hands. Matthew

133

grabbed a silver spoon and banged on a water glass. Mortified, his mother wrestled away the spoon as Matthew kicked, squirmed and tried to wriggle free. Miss B remained silent, rapidly fingering her brooch. Sam became intent on scrubbing a spot of jam from his lapel.

Oh, no! thought Rachel. Nobody is being themselves. "Everything," she loudly exclaimed, "is so delicious!"

"Oh, yes! Simply wonderful," agreed her mother.

"Great, just great," added her father.

"Sam deserves most of the credit," replied Miss B.

Rachel bragged, "Sam's cooking is almost as good as his gardening. You should see him with plants!"

Mr Szeghetti grinned. "I gather my daughter is also quite a gardener – planting the seeds of friendship."

The ice broke. Miss B agreed. "She is a truly amazing child. I can only imagine the satisfaction you must feel."

Mr Szeghetti set down his tea cup and declared, "When I saw her courage – to keep in character and hold the show together – I thought I was going to bust. I've done a lot of performing in my day, and I'll tell you, I'm not sure I could have pulled *that* off! She is quite a girl."

Miss B smoothed a few wisps of hair. "I didn't realize you were an actor."

"Well, I wouldn't go so far as to call myself that. I did a lot of plays in high school and had a few roles in a small theatre company. But money was tight, and you know how things are, a man has to earn a living. An actor's life is no way to raise a family. Now the world's my stage! Do you know what happened the other day in Shelbyville?"

Rachel smiled. Her father was off on one of his stories. Matthew contentedly hid in his tent beneath the table as Rachel fed him cakes. This led to a recounting by Miss B of an adventure under bright Sahara canopies. Soon they were all laughing, exchanging tales. Miss B told of glamorous cities and exotic places and Rachel's father told of country roads and hilarious situations.

Rachel listened intently until, "I can't stand it! I've got to run. Everything is too wonderful!" Leaping over a row of daffodils, she skipped through the powdery sweet corridor of tall box hedge. Pink and white fairy land, the garden bloomed with azaleas, dogwoods and dainty jasmine.

Birds were chirping, swooping from tree to tree. "Caw! Caw!" called a crow, flying high.

"My tulip! My mouse-tulip!" Rachel cried, racing to the far garden, remembering how she had followed this same path in winter.

The cherub in the bird–bath still smiled. The maple was now in full leaf. Rachel knelt down. There bloomed the tulip – red and radiant.

"Hello, my beautiful mouse-tulip." Rachel touched its polished petals. "You've changed and I have too. But I'll never forget you. Never."

She blew a kiss and patted the moist, spring ground.